D1743783

I believe in you

James was born in England, 1979. *Snowflakes are when angels cry* is his second novel.

Also by the author: *The Dark Paper Machine*

ISBN 978-0-9559387-0-2

James Ecendance

SNOWFLAKES
ARE WHEN
ANGELS CRY

Idearich Ltd

Buy all James Ecendance novels online at
www.idearich.com

FIRST EDITION
Released 9.9.9

Published by Idearich Ltd 2009
Festival House, GL50 3SH, England

Copyright © James Ecendance, 2009
All rights reserved

James Ecendance asserts the moral right to be identified
as the author of this work

This book is sold subject to the condition that it shall not,
by way of trade or otherwise, be lent, resold, hired out or
otherwise circulated without the publisher's prior consent
in any form of binding or cover other than that in which it
is published and without a similar condition including this
condition being imposed on the subsequent purchaser

Printed in England

ISBN 978-0-9559387-1-9

999

Chapter 1

the storm

The sound of the storm was like a roaring ocean swell that would re-carve beaches overnight. The roar gave me a backdrop for my thoughts to roam big skies and calibrate my adventure barometer.

For a moment I was the guy pulling the sled to an arbitrary magnetic point on the globe. For a moment I was the guy future girlfriends would look upon feeling cute-small and protected, as if called upon to do so, this man, their man, could chop down a great tree and splinter it for family provision.

The bone-crack of another rock fall snapped me out of make-believe-motion-picture-land and tethered me to the sinking reality of the situation; we were half way up the mountain known locally as 'The Big', or to me as 'My End'. We were half way up the mountain, sheltering on a ledge not as wide as the floor of the tent and we had been there for two days; now into a second night due to the unrelenting white-out blizzard.

In big mountain terms, two days was not a long time, but we had expected to be up and down in daylight and sat in front of the fire in the hotel telling stories of conquests of every kind, gloriously embellished with a scent from everyone's unique make-believe-motion-picture-land.

The storm had struck suddenly. Everything accidental does. Glass does not creep apart; it shatters.

The first night had been bathed in optimism. We had had torch battery power then, ate chocolate from old-school foil wrappers of crafted quality and drank coffee still warmer than our lips; heated up by gas in the car park.

Now the coffee was cold and we were not five, but four.

Chapter 2

taken

Espen's sleeping bag was still occupying tent space, huddled in the arms of his anaphylactic-stricken girlfriend, Andrea. My only public explanation was that a call of nature had taken him outside of the tent and we could rule out that he was still trying to find the right leaves.

He was gone.

Andrea was clinging to the hope that he was still alive in a snow-cave, ruing not filling a plastic bottle in the tent. But I knew he had no chance. I had seen him leave the tent – the image made-up of fragmented silhouettes, added to by tent door vibrations and a blast of cold air.

He had been naked. I had been acutely aware of that fact the moment I had woken-up to an outline against the pre-dawn sky. One remembers nakedness, shelved in memory folders of joy and horror.

He had chosen to leave and not return. He had chosen to leave Andrea alone, clinging to his sleeping bag, long extinguished of body heat, pretending that he would still be the man to gather the winter fuel and keep the home stove burning all winter long, warming the family unit. It would be a long time before she recognised that this was not to be the man destined to gather her winter fuel any longer.

That night I accepted I had lost a great friend; the kind of friend untainted by style and geography. That night I accepted that I had failed as a friend for him to walk off a mountain ridge in a snow storm wearing nothing but other men's envy.

Chapter 3

rescue

The sound of the helicopter awoke me. At first I had thought it was my washing machine taking upon itself the responsibility of my laundry. The cold stickiness of three-day old clothes reminded me that I was not home in Oslo, thinking about showering and preparing my look for the city streets.

The wilderness air greeted me as I unzipped the tent flap. A shower to my face. For a moment I enjoyed breathing in the clear air drawn from the metallic blue sky.

The blizzards were gone. They had left much but taken away more. For the first time in several days, I had a perspective on my global position. The ledge was narrow and the way down even steeper than I had thought it had been on the way up; now drowned in several metres of powder snow.

"The helicopter!" I reminded myself. I could have just sat there looking into the bleak mountain beauty for the entirety of the morning, having forgotten about the reason for opening the tent.

The helicopter was a little higher than our ledge, circling between peaks. It was searching for something. I hoped it was searching for us.

In my dreams I flew helicopters and braved storms-of-the-century to be The One. The one to bring rescue. In reality, I was perched on a mountain ledge, waving two mess-tins in the low sunlight in my orange Helly Hansen jacket. I now knew why I had bought an orange one. Most thought it was because that was the colour a sale item came in, but I now knew differently. A more stylish colour, a colour blended to the tones of ice and granite might not have caught a pilot's side-gaze.

The helicopter turned sharply and the rotor blades flexed with urgency. The rescue had begun.

Chapter 4

survivors

The winch-line coiled like a bungee rope flung from a bridge. Andrea, Nielsen and Sara were already onboard as the wind stirred from sleep. I looked at the line a few metres away and back at the tent. I had to think about it, but the tent would have to stay and become a part of the decay of the mountain. I clipped into the line and swung into the gravity-defying abyss. The helicopter had started its descent before I touched its skin.

It wasn't until I was hauled in through pepper-spray winds that I realised why.

The beeping sound signified imminent loss of engines through the lack of fuel. The pilot's voice was stern. Serious makes me comfortable. Stern was not associated with confidence in there being enough fuel to get us safely home.

"Thank you," I screamed over the hydraulic whine of the engines.

I had been the one who had rung for help that first night. The connection had been barely audible but I knew I had spoken to someone and told of our predicament. Since that moment no mobile phone had worked. There had been no signal on any network.

"Have you been looking for us for a long time?" I continued, feeling that we were the cause of excessive air-time and insufficient fuel supply.

"I wasn't looking for you at all," replied the pilot.

"Who were you looking for?"

"I was searching for anyone. You are the first ones I have found who are left...We might be the only survivors."

Chapter 5

only survivors

Where there had once been the walls and roofs of lonely log cabins were now just estuaries of storm-blown snow, burying everything in its flow. I could see the car park; moreover, the mobile phone mast which had been on the road next to the car park and therefore that was where what was left of the car park had to be. My Audi could not be seen from above, not even the shadows signifying its burial location.

My mind turned to Sunday night when I had thought we would have arrived back in Oslo. I had already begun to construct the words when stood in front of Espen's parents. It had gone unsaid, but the task would befall me as his oldest, closest friend.

I knew of every secret and of every disgrace, which now too had to be buried.

Andrea still had her face pressed to the glass, looking desperately across the various shades that white can be.

"Are you sure you can't circle across the ridge? That would be the most likely place he could have taken shelter," I asked the pilot again.

Through the fifty percent opacity ghost reflection in the glass, I saw Andrea's eyes close tightly as the same response came with an acidic burning tone.

"Your friend won't be found. He is one of The Lost now, just like my wife. I woke the first night of The Storm to find the bed sheets folded to one side where she had been lying and the draft from the back door was rattling everything that had a destiny to rattle. I stood on our doorstep and could see her footprints entering the deep snow around the house. After three steps, they were gone. She was taken by The Storm I tell you. Just like your friend, just like all the others in the village."

Chapter 6

the old miner

It was the summer without rain. That is how I remember it. A week of unbroken sunshine in a place normally with unrelenting rain. As with all trips with Espen, it had involved a scent of adventure. Something was simply not worth doing if there was no chance of losing more than dignity.

Midnight had just passed and the slight chill in the breeze had justified Espen wearing the woolly hat with sequins. The sequins were pink, as too the wool. Everything inappropriate to any mountain, summer or winter, was embroidered in its being. But this was Espen, he had found it in his parent's cottage. It belonged to a sister or his mother and was as much a part of our mountain experience as the views. Everyone else on the mountain would look upon us as the city-mountaineers, not even the rich city-mountaineers with all the gear, just city-mountaineers looking to make a new Facebook album. But beneath Espen's hopeless floral hat and my lack of waterproof clothing of any kind was our friendship, a friendship built upon moments of getting lost and not leaving each other and talking about loved ones that were battling against the ravages of life's worst curses of disease. We were built of something else. A bond that had seen us defeat enemies together, even though we added up to little on our own.

I was now on my own. The person who had understood me best, so much so as to need to say the least, had left me to find the path alone.

On that summer night, we had trekked up stony paths from the old cottage to a disused mining station. In the moonlight, no roofs could be seen to be still intact. It had been disused for a long time. But through that calm, windless night, we could hear a man at work; breaking slate. A regular tap of a chisel from beside us in one of the buildings. We said nothing but knew that we were not welcome in that place, that we were not allowed to disturb the ghost of a man lost in the mine shaft and now forever at work, breaking slate, never having peace. Of course, it could have been an animal, or a curious combination of dripping water and what lay beneath the drip, but our friendship was built on scents of adventure and that time became The Time we were almost taken by The Old Miner, to join him in his given task of breaking slate for eternity, stuck between life and death.

As the rotor blades whipped up the loose powder snow into a vortex in the air, the revolutions slowed and my path narrowed into one route; the narrowest route taking me to life or death. Within moments the velocity required to withstand gravity and keep the helicopter-magic-trick going would not be sufficient.

I was on my own and so I braced the seat in front, pushing my nose deep into the hard, non-responsive leather. If I survived, I wished to do so without a broken nose, a bodily protrusion snapped as easily as twigs on branches in storms.

I felt the moisture gathering on my forehead with the close proximity to the leather and the volume of blood thrusting through capillaries at a rhythm as fast as the blades revolved.

This was not meant to be my way. Everyone has a way to die that befits them. For some, it's bad luck. For some, it's good luck for others. For me, I was meant to just slip through the back door as that was my entrance to the world and therefore my method of exit. It would somehow be wrong to die a sudden explosive death; a death befitting a man who entered life through the front door, so that all saw the entrance. If I was to die in The Storm, it should have been by the slow onset of suppressive cold; to fade away, just like the heat.

Fuel vapours burnt dry; terminal blood loss for machines. As the engine noise was replaced by the silence bridging flight and impact, I knew it might hurt, I knew that my package, the human version of bubble-wrap might pop in places, but I knew that this was not the quiet back door. Either I was not the man I had always felt to be, that lurking beneath was my opposite twin, or I had more time to find the path. I didn't know who owned the path. It could have been God, but I seemed to like to think that it was me, otherwise God surely took my friend.

Chapter 7

LAX

I was in an airport; with check-in desks and conveyor belts for bags – there is nothing else like it on earth. This airport felt different though. The hum, like from the jet engines of the aircraft they serve, was missing, absent. The sound was lost or I was lost as I wondered around the terminal looking for someone, anyone. I knew it was my body as I recognised my feet – the feet with chiropodist-scaring toes of magnitude to make all smart shoes uncomfortable.

I was wearing no shoes and I did not recognise my clothes. I seemed to have on an iridescent orange jumpsuit. In my hands was a sealed cardboard box. I was holding it as if it was all I owned.

Looking for instruction and help, I found none and continued to walk the length of the terminal. It wasn't a cavernous public space with shops and circulating light. I wasn't in Europe; I was in an American airport with the confined space regime of designated-carrier-check-in. I chose to define it as

LAX as I needed a neurone to fire into life and record something tangible and begin to fathom out if this was my after-life, if I was meant to know which check-in desk and gate I was able to take to my God. Perhaps this was life's purpose, to know your onward flight plan from the coordinates of your current journey. But every check-in desk was lifeless and I may not have even been in Los Angeles. That was simply the only American airport my viscous memory could recall.

The only noise in the building was the friction-induced monotone of the escalators leading to departures. This caught my attention as there was nothing else displaying any vitals. A man dressed the same as me emerged at the top of the down escalator.

His jumpsuit was just as orange, the orange of a good Clementine, where the skin is still tort to the segments. He had seen me at once, standing there, canoodling with my cardboard box. He did not run but walked with a speed equal to the escalator. His hair was shaved to hide premature baldness stripes of a twenty-something and his face was beige; in colour and in looks, neutral and generic.

"Do you know where we are to go?" he asked me with anxiety pitch in his voice, a voice which had spent some time in silence.

He too held a cardboard box and I could see a label on its underside. My eyes focused on the blocky Courier font of an era when computers made everything look like space-invaders.

"Hellveta, gate six," I read and as my fingers touched the black and white label, an ice-cold sense shot through my skin and everything turned white.

"Nikolai!"

I could hear voices calling my name; voices which brewed an aroma of familiarity. I was lying face-down in the snow and I could smell burnt metal. Moreover, the oil that tends to cling to the surface of metals could be smelt.

Chapter 8

alone

Always when I thought about it, that exact thing I didn't want to happen would happen; my arm would lurch forward and swipe the mobile phone off the table sending it crashing to a hard floor. The case would separate, together with the sim card and battery and my arms would raise to the heavens; in the opposite direction to the offending random bodily reflex – as if that would prove quantum physics right and turn back time, to a time when the mobile phone was still on the table and intact.

I wished to be taken back to a time when I was waiting for the next snooze on the alarm; on a dozy Sunday morning with stillness akin to a nuclear holocaust event. I closed my inner mind, full of pictures of an unknown airport and an unnamed man trying to find his way to a place of rest and I opened my eyes to the time after the mobile casing had cracked – after the helicopter crash.

The pilot was being carried by Sara and Andrea. Blood covered his face and neck. I knew it was blood as it formed distinct island shapes among the skin-ocean. Nielsen touched my arm. I studied his beard. There were many things I hadn't done in my life and growing a professor beard was one of them.

"Can you get up?" he asked in a firm tone. Any time for his usual laidback approach had past.

"Yes, just dizziness, I must have lost consciousness for a moment."

I was pulled to my feet which were once again strapped into leather and rubber. Something clicked out of place, or back into place.

"The helicopter took the brunt of it," said Nielsen, "It won't be flying us home and that includes the pilot. He's in a bad way. He's coughing up blood, some internal injury. We have to get help as there is no one here to help us."

He pointed at the hotel, the red wooden slats built upon blocks hewn from the mountain, all slightly different shapes, but fitting into a uniform foundation of stone. When we had left out of its front door, climbers and hikers were mixing journeys and aromas, checking out or booking in for a shower. The yellow front door was wide open and drifted snow had corniced around it. The door had been left open during The Storm.

"There is no one there. A full hotel is now empty."

I followed in the wake of Nielsen's shadow. It turned the crystal surface of the snow into soot. The shadow dirtied it or showed the snow up for what it really was. For it was the light that made it like crystal, without light the snow was no more radiant than the leather of my shoes compressing it as if a mattress; the leather absorbing all from its environment including moisture.

Just as I reached the top of the steps to the front door, the wind sent a shockwave, ripping snowflakes from their sanctuary of insulating each other against inevitable melt and death for an ice crystal. The diamond dust curled through the air like steam from an underlying geyser.

The storm was brewing again. The crystal cloth of the morning sun on the snow was just a screen behind which lurked a new enemy. Nielsen had walked straight inside, his stride slicing through the tail of the drift across the doorstep. His mind was focused on the action plan; his action plan. He was going to check the phone lines, internet, and find a mobile still pumped with ions. He was convinced there was no one here to help.

By the front door there was even snow extruded from the top of the cigarette bin. Part of the snow had been cast aside, perhaps by a bird or gravity, but I caught the slightest tinge of ash in the filter-clean mountain air. Someone had been smoking a cigarette just before the helicopter crash. They would have heard it. They would have been drawn to carry the injured and tear a morsel from the bread of human suffering.

I was also convinced there was no one here to help; no one who wanted to help us.

Chapter 9

secret

Nielsen was leant over the reception computer as I stood in the doorway. The seat by the entrance usually occupied by someone with a tale and a coffee was empty, but the cushion was ruffled, in the way hair is by a lover. No one had straightened the ruffles out. The normal cycle of things had been interrupted in a hurry.

Nielson shook his head and the mouse. It rattled as if a baby was vigorously exploring the wondrous world of repetitive sound. It did not matter that some electronic innards were floating around in the cyber cerebral fluid. It would not have mattered if the mouse had been unplugged.

There was no Internet.

The two little computers in the menu bar had the red cross of barren bytes. We were disconnected from the world. Nielsen plucked up the reception phone but his arm motion slowed as it neared his ear.

That reaction meant there was no dial tone. For the first time I saw the lines of weathering on his face as everything scrunched up with anxiety – forehead, eyes and mouth.

For someone who casually past over life as a surf board transcends a Hawaiian wave, it was an unusual feeling for him; the heat acupuncture of tension. He glared at me. As if by doing nothing, it was all my doing.

But I had seen that the phone had already been off the hook and the screensaver had not yet kicked in after the ubiquitous fifteen minutes of rejection.

Someone had already been trying to find an Internet and phone connection, and that fact was more important than there not being any connectivity at all.

Why didn't I say anything? Things might have turned out differently if we all had known, if we all had been prepared. But I shrugged at Nielson, partly fixated by the change in his character; from the confusion brought on by The Storm, or the realisation that if we were all that was left then he had made his choice already – Sara was his for eternity. Knowing more than Nielsen made me feel a little empowered. It gave me wisdom when he had always been the wise. No longer was he the effortless athlete and effortless Lothario to me. In the new post-storm kingdom, I would be King – always with a greater knowledge of the new world gained by careful observation, overlooked as being uninterested in the people around.

"Help, we can't stop the bleeding!"

My kingdom crumbled. It was nothing without kinsmen. There was panic in Sara's voice from the kitchens behind reception. My thoughts of arming myself with a knife disappeared as our pilot, the man we owed our lives to, bled to death on a stainless steel counter more akin to sushi preparation.

We were now forever his mortal servants; his blood loss opposed by our heightened blood pressure.

Chapter 10

plasma

When I was younger, life was all about what I might be; what I had the skills-in-waiting for and what my dreams stirred inside the ribcage housing the machine of potential. Now life was about what I was, my current GSM coordinates and after that it would just be about my log – the data of what my dreams became and where I ended up.

That was not supposed to happen to us; Espen and me. We were supposed to be the exception, somehow immune to all the cell destroying free radicals that would strip us of our ability to be young and think like a young person.

Our life-log was never to be complete. At eighty, we were still going to be getting to the top of a peak many before had trodden, but pretending that the path we were on had been previously hidden to our generation and now we had discovered the route of the ancients, not the well-beaten paths of guide books and lines of trudging trekkers with at least one umbrella between them.

The pact against the onset of bodily dysfunction and dementia had been broken, broken by Espen.

What pressure had driven him to walk out into certain death in the middle of The Storm? What terrible thought had preceded the desire to live out new thoughts?

The omnipresent darkness of the basement held onto its wisdom.

The only light I could find was in the stairwell and the door pulled itself shut with venom akin to spurned lust. A correctly placed fire extinguisher filtered the light through the propped open door into the basement expanse, making halogen seem like candlelight. Sara needed blood plasma. As a base station for mountain rescue, I presumed their first aid kit might have been better equipped than the average plaster - scissors - headache pill combo, somehow combining to treat severe trauma.

The first aid kit in the kitchen had been ominously bare; the mirror on the cabinet door had taken up the most space, reflecting the solemn stone-tooled expression of Sara having had the task of saving the pilot's life put upon her as the student nurse.

Her reflection in the mirror had told the story of the grim reality that hits everyone at some point, the reality that old-age is not the right we previously believed, but a privilege handed out randomly and if a seemingly good man, a man who had found and settled with his love, a man who had achieved career goals and challenges remaining secret to probably all; if a man like that was on the brink of death then anyone could die such.

"Where is God today?" I mumbled, thinking of Espen and the longevity of that event; forever without my friend, forever without sharing the concentrate of life - pressed, pureed and reduced to a rich flavoursome hit among blandness.

"On holiday? Having a little break in His villa in Malaga?"

"Or maybe we are the ones on holiday, have you thought about that? That this is just a break from our usual home..."

The answer came from the man I had seen in my dreams of LAX, standing to one side of a stone pillar

31

in the 10% cyan. Still, in such low light the orange jumpsuit projected forth.

"How are you here? You were just in my dream? Are you the surviving guest?"

"I am the one with questions for you stranger - what were you doing in our world? The Storm did not choose you to travel to The New Place. You died in your tent and now must find your own way home before the soldiers of hell reoccupy their land."

I rubbed my throbbing head, caked dry blood like the first heavy frost of an early Autumn flaked away towards my feet. The man wasn't there anymore and my ears felt blocked, the same way in which they become uncomfortably tight on aircraft descent; the pressure of reality returning from the tinned paradise of mid-air isolation. The helicopter crash had clearly disrupted my comprehension of what was real and make-believe. I had become a two year old child again; where fever induced nightmares appear real as all is real at that age.

The man in the orange jumpsuit was gone, but his cardboard box clearly remained, lying on the concrete, surrounded by dust as if it had always been there. I peeled back the tape and label marked *Hellveta* and the cardboard flap sprang up.

Inside, I found blood plasma.

Chapter 11

found

A humming bird feeds on the rich nectar of flowers, but not everything flowers year-round or every year. Flowers all around were dying. The rhythm of beating wings receding.

The door to the store cupboard was locked.

"We should find candles and anything to keep us warm. The Storm isn't finished yet."

"Why Nikolai?" asked Sara, finally sitting down on a kitchen stool, after her time collecting nectar in the clover field. The blood had soaked through to her skin and it was now only warmed from her body. "Your melancholy will not help us now. We have electricity and warmth; we are safe but the pilot is not. He needs a hospital; I can only warm his blood for so long."

"You heard what the pilot said; that everyone is missing. We have to wake-up and understand that

Espen was not the only one...to venture into The Storm. Perhaps we are now the only ones left."

Andrea stared at me in silence. She didn't want Espen mentioned, she didn't want the truth of him taking his own life revealed; for that interrupted the life they were still sharing within her, where he hugged as granite and she crumbled as sand.

"We have no definitive evidence that anyone else is missing. The only fact is that there has been a storm, fierce enough to have evacuated the hotel and blocked the roads used to the weight of winter."

"Let's hope so," I replied to Sara, looking at the light bulb over us, still burning brightly; the nectar to our beat.

The timbers and glass shook as if a wave had passed over what was now our life raft. The Storm was on its way back. The clouds outside, illuminated by the gentle September afternoon light, were black and overloaded with snow crystals. Strange that something so white could create something so dark. For a moment I was back in Grünerløkka, walking the peaceful streets not yet disturbed by the optimum fifteen second espresso rush. I would wander early while my alarm clock and shower whimpered lonely, my attention given to the authority of the city; king over the land, framing the distant sky that could not touch us. Those days I was thankful for the time pre-breakfast, for the time when losing track of everything important kept hunger away.

Sara held her forehead in her hands. "I should be visiting my grandmother this afternoon; she will be expecting us..."

She shook her head and turned her concentration away from her own concerns and back to the pilot. Her grandmother was gravely ill, I knew that and I knew it caused her pain, that she lived in a cage of pain, unable to walk the city streets pre-breakfast with the door to worry locked shut. She could not ease her grandmother's suffering; old-age was playing its hand.

It was at that moment, while I wondered how to break down the locked door and find candles and blankets to ease suffering; carried and to come, that Nielsen made his discovery, or we became aware. 3.16 in the afternoon, as Sara and Andrea battled against the slow creep of loss, dampening all happiness inertia.

His dark beard twitched - the underlying muscles normally hidden, revealing themselves to be full of nervous fluid.

"I have found a body in one of the hotel rooms. I don't know how they died, but they died naked. The walls were covered in writing. They were writing instructions, a map. A map of how to get out of here."

"Back to the village?"

"To heaven; his writing said that The Storm is not a storm, it's the oncoming of hell."

Chapter 12

white horse

Sara was the first to get to the room; the master suite on the third floor with views of the mountain peak we had been stranded on half way up. She had to be certain for herself that the man was dead. Death is not something all are familiar with, just as with hanging curtains. Sara had to check they were level when Nielsen had put up the rail and so now, she had to check there was a flat line as well.

Was this the person that I knew was in the hotel from the cigarette smoke when we had first arrived? My stomach found its stage calling and released heavy stones into my intestine. If this was that same person, they had probably been alive when they heard our helicopter and if we had all searched the hotel for them straight away, the heaviest of stones that take you to death might have been delayed.

But I had kept knowledge to myself and the man was now a lifeless avatar.

The question everyone wanted to ask was how he had died. But no one did. The cool air that comes with silence enveloped the room.

There was no bloodshed. The dagger had struck from within. That brought fear, for if it was something he ate, we had no choice but to eat the same and if it was a virus, we had already breathed the same air for too long.

The sheets were pulled over his body. There was nothing else we could do than close the door behind us and hope that the next people to open it commanded authority. Nielsen had glanced over the writings that covered the wall nearest the window with the mountain view. I took a moment to memorise it too. These had been the last thoughts of a man who had interacted with the knit of our lives, changing the pattern ever so slightly forever and so could not be just dismissed; a knit cannot be undone. The lines of wool define the path we have taken and what form it can become. A sock can never be a jumper to more than a mouse.

The Storm has taken those who were marked. The trial now begins. The Storm will never relent for it blows hell ward. The only path to heaven is to follow the white horse that will guide you home.

I locked the door; not vibrant enough to be green but more interesting than beige. My mind was still full of thoughts of poisoned food and air-born illness, but there were new nebula forming. Had Espen seen a white horse? I wanted to believe he was riding in the mountains on a white horse and not sat shattered in tissue and bone at the foot of the second ice field after being too overwhelmed with life to be able to live.

I wanted it so much, but there were no horses in these mountains. Some reindeer in Spring, but no horses.

"We have a picture. There is a TV channel broadcasting!"

The vision of Espen, my friend who had come to me from the land of giants, on his white horse faded. His blond hair and doubt defeating smile were the last things to fade. I stood on the landing, half of the screen was blocked by the door into the library, but I could see the revolving images nonetheless. Dots of red, green and blue, beamed from one place to another, starred upon as if the very origins of life.

It was news, looking at finances, followed by some world conference with flags of nations in front. Life was happening as normal around us. The Storm was an isolated event, not a global judgment. The people of the hotel and high villages would be in the lowlands, sorting out a way back to where they came from, either the villages that belonged to the mountains or the cities that belonged to the sea.

That image of people strengthened by soup in polystyrene cups in gymnasium gatherings faded also. Everyone's luggage was still in the hotel, left as if they didn't expect to leave. There was only one road down the valley, the same route that the glacier which paved the path would have taken centuries before. And now the snow had returned to its natural habitat to block the exit all would have needed to have driven eleven kilometres down - to where the roots of the mountains entered the soil.

There was also the man in room three hundred and three. Late twenties with a shaven head to pretend that the train of baldness wasn't picking up speed to its final destination. All he was missing was an iridescent orange jumpsuit. This was the man I had seen in my delirium post-crash.

This was the man from LAX.

Chapter 13

the islands

Their bodies had squeezed the air from its secret hiding place in the sofa, to run the risk of being sucked into jet engine lungs and having its oxygen permanently removed. Tension in muscles dissolved into lessening blood streams and previously tort flesh became sofa-like. The status quo had returned for there was television before their eyes. The green light of human normality. The sign that someone was home; the soup bubbling gently on the Aga with today's newspaper open at page seven on the kitchen table.

But the status quo was taking a day off through my eyes. The green light was blinking. Someone was home, but whose home we were in I did not know. The dull ache echoed into my skull to become a sharp pain. I had once tripped as a child and head-butted a wall. Back then I had had immediate motherly attention, rubs and blasts of fresh air down the hill from my village on a bicycle. Natural medicine for my hurt.

I had no bicycle this time for the breeze to run its fronds over my scalp and peel away throbbing pain. The pressure was just building up in my damaged brain. I could have been comatose now and dreams not following the thin thread of time. So I could have seen the man dead in the bed before meeting him in the hazy white airport. I could have been back in Oslo a year after The Storm and helicopter crash, reliving things one disturbed night, or maybe I never woke up from the helicopter impact at all. Unknown faces could be feeding me and washing my butt; hoping I would wake up and give the bed to someone else.

It felt like I was sat down but I didn't remember sitting, I couldn't remember how I got to many places.

The seat was leather; leather made for regular use - to last a long time, maybe longer than it lived.

"I've got you a coffee," he said as I lifted the vending cup of polystyrene nourishment to my lips. Warm but not hot.

"I'm Nikolai by the way."

I looked at the bald man, now flush with life in his face and coffee in his stomach.

"Arlanda, nice to meet you Nikolai. I think we are going to be here some time."

He pointed at the departure screen with his orange clad arm. All flights were delayed.

"Do you know where we are going Arlanda?"

I was surprised that the airport appeared to be real and there was a possibility to find my way to another place, perhaps off the mountain, or back there.

"The lady at the check-in desk sorted me out. I just gave in my cardboard box and I received a boarding pass to The Islands. I asked for two tickets, but she said she only had one."

"Where is she?"

"Still there, at the far end, the only check-in desk occupied. I had time to explore every nook when you disappeared before. You must have had a bad stomach or something I guess as one moment we were talking and then you had gone and left me alone when I had already been on my own for a long time."

I found myself walking across the floor that looked like marble, but was not, was some plasticised version of the real thing. I did not even know if I had told my body to do it, to leave the comfort of the chair behind and expose myself in the empty space, void of other human passage. But then I had never told my legs to bend at the knee and sit down in the first place.

You have no control over your body in dreams. Things happen. You follow the sprocket holes in the Kodak.

She was somewhere within the age when a woman is young. Perhaps that is always the age similar to your own; years ago she would have been old to me, like a teacher, with lines where things previously hadn't needed to crease.

Frida

She wore a badge perfectly positioned in the area not definable as her shoulder, not left enough to be her arm and not right enough to be her breast plate, nor low enough to be where badges do not belong; perfectly positioned over the name-and-job-position-tarsal, given freedom to move by the phalangeal badge. The fact that she was named by something

45

higher gave me peace. It meant that something else was in control, that if I lashed out too much in my dream no one would get hurt as rules were governing the playing field. People had names and job titles.

Frida. Flight Attendant, Welken Airways

She blinked, or I blinked, either way shutters drooped over the shop window from heavy rain before pooling too long in one place and collapsing earthward to start life roaming the gutter.

I could see an eye lash on the shiny check-in counter. I never saw it fall to its resting place. It just appeared; the rarest of all hairs. Endangered. We cannot ever afford to lose too many in too short a time, so it was placed among my memories of things we glimpse seldom. The person who delivers newspapers to all the shops. The rain that falls when we sleep. Eye lashes of perfect sickle moon shape.

I wanted to pass on luggage to Frida and take a journey on Welken Airways but she shook her head and my own head had already glanced at my empty, air-rated hands without me thinking to check. I had lost my cardboard box too.

"I have no seats available at present for this flight," she said with authority, but the way someone has authority in declaring muffins to be baked and ready to be removed from the oven. Authority that makes you feel at home.

"Are you sure, can you check again? You had a seat for Arlanda?"

"There are no other seats at present. He had already booked his travel with us. You haven't booked, we have to find a place for you and you have to know where we travel to."

"The Islands..."

"The Islands, with long sandy beaches in perfect sheltered bays; the vault of heaven to some, and right now, you are not welcome, and do not even believe you are standing at its check-in gates. You have to lead your people out of the mountains before the second storm comes. You have little time. They must find the white horse. You have little time. The first storm fell from the sky, the second storm will rise from the earth."

The television blinked. The black screen of no signal exposing dust veneer before illuminated pixels returned.

Chapter 14

not alone

Sara was holding my neck, perhaps trying to keep my head up as my focus weaved a jumper or new socks capable of withstanding winter cold or keeping toes pink and refreshed by blood in every day temperate apartments.

"How long have I been out?"

"You just sat down. Have you passed out before, are you feeling dizzy?"

"I've spent ten minutes somewhere else. I'm not sure if I was awake or sleeping, or that I could feel my toes. The airport was cold."

Concern swept across Sara's face; the inner breeze taking hold. Her hand moved up to shield external forces. Fingers used to taking onboard other's pain drew circles as if sand replaced my skin. Her tanks were filled yet again. A capacity for storing hurt so it did not have to be carried by those not strong enough to do so. But where was her hurt stored? Was there a tank buried deep for her own darts that strike with surprise? Fired in darkness. Tipped with bad news.

Espen had been her friend too. She knew him through Nielsen, they met because Nielsen knew Espen first, but no one really just knows someone through someone else. The clay that we form impressions out of belongs to us. We knead it and add moisture. We bake it hard and break it at the most brittle points.

Feelings are the most independent states. Partnerships can be formed but none can be governed by another state.

"I think you have concussion from the crash Nikolai. You must rest. Find a hotel room and try to sleep. It looks like we are here for the night and we have everything we need to be comfortable. I don't think you need Visa for a room."

"If I close my eyes I am taken to this airport and the man we found dead in the hotel room is there, waiting for his plane to The Islands, a place of apparent beauty. His name is Arlanda and he gave me the blood plasma that saved the pilot's life, except then he did not seem the same, he was angry and told me that we all died in the tent on the mountain and this is our afterlife."

Sara sighed. A tank was full to the brim, perhaps a little ran down the side, leaving a trail that would take a while to dry in the still air.

"You have a head injury Nikolai. The brain is a fragile thing and it can play illusions on us when ill. You can see things you feel are real and time can run fast or slow. You could have a fracture. Pressure might be building on your brain but it also might be a light knock. If you have nausea or more of these black outs then you have to tell me, but when help can get through the snow drifts...you'll be fine, whatever has happened inside that head of yours..."

Sara smiled. Her blonde hair that had been touching my face rippled from the onset of the smile. If I had fractured my skull and the snow drifts were impassable then my fate would be entwined with my new acquaintance, Arlanda.

As I lay my head down in room seventeen, the wind began to rattle at the windows. Usually I found it comforting, to know that I was just a part of something that had survived millennia without me guiding it. Tonight, it wasn't a comforting sound as snow dripped down the glass, striking it almost horizontally. For two days The Storm had raged while we ate all of the chocolate we possessed and now we had a supply of chocolate once more, but it didn't taste the way it had when shared with five.

I was tired. I could feel the extra kilograms it brings; increasing the density of bones. An organic alchemy. Even though my muscles had lain idle for two days in the womb of the mountain, sleep hadn't been easy. I wasn't used to oxygen being shared, to be able to hear its narrow passage from cavern to cave.

But sleep was still not easy. From the window I could occasionally see the peak of Storen and its many sharp edges, but only when the wind swirled upward and parted otherwise relentless snowfall. A mountain at night pushes black to new depths, it's darker, more light-zapping than any human equivalent, be it on paper or when the curtains are drawn and door to the corridor closed.

I wanted to be at home, to be among my things that had a home but were rarely put away, to be able to see a film that my memory knew pieces of; enough to not be surprised by the story twists. A place I wanted to be least was still in the tent that had been left for the wild ones to play in.

A gladness grew. As if an astronaut re-entering the atmosphere, a heavier and heavier gravity tugged me back to the white sheets. We were lucky to have made it down to the hotel. I began looking forward to resting and starting the healing process on the underside of my skull and banishing Arlanda and LAX to my memories of that day on the mountain.

I turned; ready to accept the relinquishing of responsibility that sleep demands.

The light was a pin-prick to a needle eye. It burnt a little brighter and three more followed on behind, about where the glacier turned into moraine.

There were people on the mountain, making their way down and all ridges, scree slopes and valleys stopped at the stone steps of the hotel of mountain legend.

Two hours, maybe three and they would want a hot drink and dinner, or a lot more if these were the soldiers of hell promised by Arlanda. The mountain seemed a fitting place for their march to begin.

Chapter 15

prisoners

During the winter Norway stores up its light. A giant capacitor somewhere keeps it all away from view to dissipate it during long summer months. The cycle of life speeds up at this time. The grass sheds its winter colours and strives for the moon; its eternally optimistic target. Everything that has the feint urge, gets it stronger, to multiply before the fumbling in the darkness returns.

I longed for it to be summer, for light to shine over the mountains, glinting off minerals formed when time was a young man still with dreams of always being young and carefree. Now time had suddenly gotten older and harder to me, sending katabatic winds to erode minerals into constituent ashes. Dull and unable to glint like their brothers and sisters did. I felt that we were the minerals today, being eroded, with our potential to be diamonds reducing to black ash worthy of drainage - not even holding nutrients for soil. We were becoming The Lost; lost on the mountain.

I had always thought of us as the strongest of crystals; Espen, Nielsen, Sara, Andrea and I. A group bound by a tangled web of friendship, by choice and by association. But this had become my group; simply the most regular attendees of food grilling and waffle-embossed bums from the Frogner Park grass. They also seemed to enjoy my tales of human oddity, like the man I'd seen driving an old car, so old that it was all bulbous and weathered - both man and car. Brown, tortoise mottled dinner-plate-glasses had been worn at a forty-five degree slant and the car driven as erratically as a fairground bumper car straight into a mound of three month old compacted snow on the pavement. All would form their own stop-frame animation of the brief encounter on my drive to the Gallery Bus Terminal. They would smile picturing their Granddad at the wheel, dressed a little wonky and smelling of the potting shed in Spring.

I had settled on these people being my closest electrical connections in the circuit formed unwittingly on the journey between islands of contact. They would laugh when I laughed, even when I recited each tale for a third time non-stop, with few other notebook-worthy moments for recital. This held our connection together, even when Andrea would neurotically switch off all electrical appliances at 11.30pm on weekends away, and Espen would never settle on doing nothing over doing something ridiculous and Nielsen had never really spoken to me any deeper than aeroplane safety announcement speak. None of that mattered as we laughed together and cried together now; emotions that glint in sunlight on the surface, hinting of richer minerals buried beneath.

But now that vault of summer sunlight was empty and it was night-time with blizzard in tow, capable of taking grown men from their sleeping bags, eroding completely what I had thought too tough to disperse. I now doubted the rest of us would make it back to the city.

Ashes remain where they are blown.

There was a knock at my hotel room door as I stood pondering, still in the same place, still between window and bed where I had seen the four lights descending the mountain. Nielsen entered, without waiting for a response.

He spoke but all I heard was *stay seated and keep your seatbelt fastened until the Captain has turned the seatbelt sign off.*

And so I sat, on the corner of the bed; making a crease but not crumpling.

Nielsen held a bowl of pasta. It was for me. The only thing he had ever usually given me was a beer which I would half drink and then hide under the coffee table at a time in the party when no one would notice you weren't drinking. Suddenly I heard his words for the first time with a new clarity. He did see me as one of his closest connections. He had thought of me when food had been served, he had noticed a missing connection; Nikolai.

"The pilot is awake," he said.

The tone expressed that I needed to know. It went up, not down. A memo to your boss who will relay the decision is made in the same way.

"He is asking for you..."

"Why me? We never even introduced ourselves in the helicopter - he spoke to me as a passenger."

"Apparently while he has been unconscious you have been sharing an airport departure lounge and only you know where his ticket is. Even if you have nothing to say to him, he has to hear something - he has barricaded the doors with chairs and says The Storm will try to take us all this time. He has the fire axe. I think he would rather kill us than let us leave."

Chapter 16

the pilot

Sunlight brings out a new spectrum. It remains hidden for beautiful days. Extra greens and blues clothe the landscape.

Darkness reveals the shy shades you didn't know lived behind the glorious palette.

As I walked behind Nielsen, the corridor revealed those shy shades. The wooden panelling across the walls was no longer various shade of nut but now the colour of dying embers as if the timbers were burnt. The slightest hint of red I hadn't noticed on the way up the stairs, now had its time, its time to etch on our chromatic paper being printed in the mechanism of cogs and whirling sprockets behind our eyes.

"Nikolai!"

The pilot was at the foot of the stairs, and one of his feet proclaimed the first step as his territory, ready to climb to us if we did not descend.

Nielson let me go first, with a gentle thrust of his palm across my shoulder.

The blood on his face had blackened. His focus swung as if his eyes were tethered to a pendulum in his head. His breathing was audible from afar, probably due to the impact injury to his ribs and pooling of fluid that should flow.

"Lothen," I replied.

I didn't previously know his name. Getting the helicopter remotely down had been his priority and he had been nameless to us all, simply The Pilot. But one of the chambers of my mind had known who he was and continued the familiarity by hauling my arm from my side and shaking his bloodied hand. My body was at ease with him, even though he held the fire axe in his other hand and he had the stature of a man who could wield one and take down a tree, or another man.

"Do I know you?" You only told me about the disappearance of your village in the helicopter. We never exchanged names."

"I've just spent three hours with you in the airport, so I think we know each other quite well now. You cannot go back on your promise. You cannot break your word...to help me, to help me find her, my wife. Evelyn was taken by The Storm to The Islands and so that is where I have to go..."

"How do you know that?"

"You told me Nikolai. You told me that The Storm has taken the chosen back to The Islands, among them was my wife and you know this as you have been there, The Islands and just come back."

"Why has The Storm not killed all?"

"The Storm did not kill my wife! You have seen her alive and I was not chosen to be taken but you know how, you know how I can leave that airport as you managed it yourself..."

"The people here have to be protected and led down the mountain before the worst of The Storm strikes, led to the..."

"The White Horse."

"Exactly, but I have to do that. You must die to see Evelyn again," came from deep inside a chamber that emerged from hiding, from the past or future of my memory. No mortal task was worth dying for and I was uncomfortable with my own words. "But The Storm is back, why can't it just take us all?" I asked, not wanting to pry into my secret closet memory.

"It isn't the same storm. You warned me about it, everyone on The Islands, warned you about it, the desire we would feel to step out into it, but now you said that The Storm brings the soldiers of hell and the snowflakes are when angels cry. The soldiers will only try to tempt us to a place where our loved ones are not and that is why I am to stand guard and stop anyone going outside..."

I looked at the front door, now entombed in furniture. There were other exits. If we wanted to leave, one could run one way, and one the other, but both getting out alive couldn't be guaranteed. Lothen had the look of a fire-juggler about him. Focusing hard on not getting burnt but blackened nonetheless.

No matter how much he believed it, I couldn't have told him anything about The Islands and his wife as we had both been unconscious and in my dreams, I was seeking knowledge and hadn't acquired it, to become the giver of it.

"You have a head injury Lothen, just like me. We have been given vivid dreams of airports and ways to escape what has entrapped us. I was the last person you spoke to before we crashed, so it is no surprise that..."

His focus narrowed on me and his body stood firm and rigid.

"Easy to just call it that, but you know it was more than a dream. I don't know what The Storm is but at some point the world has to end and this seems like it to me. You made me a promise to help me get to Evelyn and in return I promised that I would help you find Natalie."

It was 1988; the class rabbit had to be looked after over the Easter holidays. Natalie and I were chosen as we sat together in class and had shared top marks that term. It meant that our parents would have to talk to each other and organise the swap halfway through the holidays. The rabbit became the symbol of our childhood infatuation with each other, separated by a holiday but joined by the responsibility of caring for the rabbit. The rabbit died the next term, we sat on different tables the next school years and twenty years had passed since we last copied each other's curly g's.

Lothen stood there having played the Natalie card well. It was then I noticed that he was still in his helicopter jumpsuit and it was orange.

"They are coming down the mountain already. At least four of them. I saw the lights," I said, nodding to Lothen.

"We have time to be prepared then. We need someone on permanent look out now. The soldiers' march will be fast."

Chapter 17

vault of heaven

The pasta was cold. Pasta loses heat seemingly faster than any other food group. Its large surface area doesn't help. Neither do the artistic shapes. Nielsen should have made soup, the lord of high heat retention, but he expected me to be hungry and to eat straight away. And I had been expecting to be sleeping; to be dreaming about summer where water flows free and the birds sing about the water's freedom. But I had looked north.

North was where winter began and summer hid.

North was where the hotel pointed. When it had been first built in the time of early exploration by men looking like miners, not climbers, it had looked south, down the valley where all the water flowed. The hotel had been rebuilt so the most expensive rooms had the perfect summit view. That was what the customers demanded, as well as pristine white sheets to be pinned under before pinning down an ascent of a pristine white slope.

Through the glass in the front hotel lounge I stared at the dark expanse of the mountain vista. There were no lights. Perhaps the contours were lying to my eyes, smuggling the four down the mountain hidden from view by the age-old undulations. Perhaps I hadn't seen anything, just the sparkle of fatigue, a short circuit in my cranium.

I knew one thing though; we couldn't stay at the hotel. It wasn't a sanctuary against The Storm, a place of shelter. The wise had left in a hurry and left their beds for those who hadn't been chosen.

On the walls I was surrounded by photographs of the generations who had long ago taken up custody of the mountains; temporarily inhabiting what would out live them all. All their faces were so stern in black and white. The grainy print removed all softness and feathering from one tone to another. Contrast was stark and moustaches ruled like no other time in human history.

Yet the mountains looked the same. They had weathered great wars, revolutions and the oncoming of colour with immunity. Perhaps their role was to provide shelter, keeping the cold away from the valleys, plains and cities; holding the storms in a cage around its slopes. But that did not make me feel safe. My body couldn't surcome to the softness of the chair, for I was not in those warmer valleys, plains and cities tonight. The people of the nineteenth century in the photographs might have felt the same at times. They had lived an unplugged life without internet messaging, phones or news bulletins. Their worlds could have come to a sudden end and they would have learnt as quickly as the hooves of horses could travel. Therefore their fate was completely delegated. Modern lives tried to reign in fate, to make everything so fast as to slow down its control. An earthquake could rock Beijing. An aircraft could fail to send its location signal and disappear from radar over ocean and instantly the world would know. Blogs would write about it. Blackberrys would blink red diodes across bedside tables, receiving the email while you slept. The impact of events could perhaps be lessened. Search teams could respond faster. Hospitals could wake their doctors and prepare, but no matter how quickly and by how many different means the news was transmitted, the event could not yet be prevented or reversed. Fate, what will happen to you outside of your control, either by simple chance, a combination of possibilities, or decreed by an unseen order - fate; cannot be contained for it has not yet occurred so you have no news of it to relay. So if there had been a working phone, or if the internet had done its thing then we may have shared our plight, we may have sent a message to Espen's parents making them sit at the dining room table holding each other and their favourite pictures, several days earlier than they now needed to endure. Nobody would have been able to reach us though.

The road was impassable and the wind too untamed for rotor blades. Fate would have its way with us nonetheless. This made me more comfortable with being trapped, both in the hotel and the airport in my head. I had to think like they did in the nineteenth century now. They had known so little yet trusted so much. A whisky might have been half empty by now, a new baby on the way in June or stories kept alive and glorified by firelight. We were only illuminated by worry. I was worried about not getting home and subsequently that meant I was worried about missing a day or two of work and not paying the bill that was waiting. Espen, he brought me worry as well, moreover torment, that I had neither saved him nor been able to search for him. And then there was Arlanda, the man who had befriended me at my imagined LAX and cursed me in the basement and the intolerable thought that it had all felt too real for a dream. I had unusually felt cold and warmth in my dreams, and now the pilot had further complicated things with his similar experience. So I worried most about letting the people down in my visions, by not getting everyone safely down the mountain and home.

The men and women dressed in clothes that must have chaffed stared out into the hotel lounge without the worry lines that etched rivulets into twenty-first century faces. One of them looked like Ian Holm, the actor you suddenly realise one day is in almost every film. He looked like the way Ian Holm would with a moustache. One rivulet of worry on my face dried up. If Ian Holm had survived isolation and storms in these mountains and returned to find The Ring, then perhaps I could trans-navigate back to The Shire.

Lothen drank his coffee like the way only Norwegians can. It seems to hydrate Norwegians; they only become stronger upon drinking it. The cup had been brought to him by Sara. Her worry lines included the pilot, included worrying that any blood clots could fall like dam walls anytime within him and of course she worried about what she saw as his delusional state. A sure sign to her of malfunction and bleeding in his brain, or an easy way to dismiss everything he said. I had told Sara about my dreams of the airport before the pilot had woken up, I wondered if deep down behind the titanium shell that let other's hurt be sheltered overnight, she had connected the two and couldn't make a medical response leading to the hurt overwhelming her. That could have been why the coffee cup had been delivered by meek hands, the coffee more to appease than to cradle.

"Tell me about your wife," I said to Lothen, wondering if she would have liked him with a moustache, if she had been a childhood love or a love that had slowly rolled his way like the stones across the mountain scree slopes.

His face could have lit a candle. The fierce frown disintegrated in an instant and I could see he was instantly with her in his mind. He was there, shovelling the snow that had built up on the steps of the basement flat; so that she could step more easily and he could feel his heart pound with every pillow of snow cast aside. He was there, seeing her through the window from the dark outside, dressed for him and waiting for when it was time for him to knock. I could sense that this love hadn't been easy; no drive-thru takeaway. Wild mountain goats had been sacrificed to quell the loathing of Carlos. Carlos is present in all relationships that endure and grow roots where previously no roots could gain hold. He is there to test us, disconnecting the Skype call, increasing the cost of plane tickets, sending your letter to his home address in Columbia instead of its true destination. It is all Carlos's doing as his mission is no longer motivated by love and ultimately any task big or small in life not motivated by love is empty. I could see it in the web of lines jetting forth from all the corners of Lothen's eyes that were now pearls. They had battled Carlos long and hard and won. They had won each other's hearts to be shared for a long time.

"She has... a wonderful smile that lights up my world, she creates a wonderful atmosphere, she has a heart of only goodness and a heart that wants to serve others. She treats her friends like closest family and she will wait patiently in cafés. Little children and babies reach out to her. I miss her even before she has left. She cuts carrots like others carve their sculptures. She appreciates simple things, the things that do not cost a lot but are full of richness. She simply makes me happy and no one ever has before, not in that way... not in that way, Evelyn..."

"Then I will take you to her. I cannot promise we'll make it, but if you do, she will be waiting, she's waiting for you to return home."

"And I will get you to Natalie..."

"I haven't seen Natalie for twenty years. She is still young in my heart. She is not the person I would choose to go to."

"We lose touch with people. Not everyone is good with rope and knots and we lose touch. But I believe that no one forgets, once you have befriended, loved in any gradient of the word, love, you will always mean something and memories can be remembered as if yesterday after eighty years. She may not be loved by you in the same way as I love Evelyn, but you were torn with sadness when we sat together at the airport..."

"What did I say? What did I say about Natalie?"

"That she wasn't there, in The Islands, that she had chosen another path. You were distraught as you remembered her as a person who was only full of goodness and therefore had to be in the place where all goodness comes from; The Islands. I will help you try to change her path."

A light blinked across the mountain ridge that separated the two glacial lakes. Under two hours now. I had turned from Lothen's face still glowing from his thoughts of Evelyn and was looking out into the expanse of black where perhaps Espen lay crumpled. The remnants only to be found by future climbers.

"And what with Espen, did I talk of him?"

"Of course. Your path is now the same as his, for his Andrea was not to be found in The Islands and you left together. I met him too, tall, blonde hair, before he left to try to find her, but..."

"But?"

"It's so difficult for me to tell you what you can't recall as I am so grateful that you will help me find my way to Evelyn but that makes me so sad too. The staff at the airport told us quite clearly that the journey to The Islands is one-way; even if you save the person you left for and get them a seat on the last plane to The Islands, I guess you cannot go with them. The next one will be the last one we were told

73

and you and Espen have chosen to give it all up for the chance that two people you hold dear may get to spend eternity in..."

"The Islands?"

"The vault of heaven."

Chapter 18

escape

"Do your sleeping on your own time."

It sounded like my boss, or a number of my bosses. If you have ever purchased a bicycle with a missing bolt on the water bottle holder, that might have been my work. Back then I needed the money, but didn't value the process of earning it. Every bolt counts. Every bolt is there for a reason.

Time in the bathroom counted as quality time to me. Especially when taken within places you didn't want to be, like a wedding where I knew no one, a work shift when all bolts did not fit their thread, or a hotel which you couldn't leave but no one would come to. And so, as usual, I took an extra few minutes to find the odd hair that been distracted by the mysterious forces that misshapen hairstyles; like wind and jumpers. The majority of the major decisions in my life were taken while repairing the damage of those mysterious forces on my appearance.

It was then it came to me, while I stared at the stubble that was becoming wild, which had become aware of its own existence after three days of surviving the life-long battle against the brutal Viking invasions of the razor.

I had seen it in one of the photographs, of men looking like miners, not climbers. It was hard to tell the two apart with the ungainly boots and pick axe that were common to both professions. The photograph *had* been of miners. These mountains had to earn a living too. We had passed it on the web-thin mountain road on the way up to the hotel - the hydroelectric plant, fed by the glacial melt waters that roared of their presence.

There was a huge network of tunnels that took water directly from the high mountains straight down the valley at the optimum angle for gravity to have its wicked way, without even anaesthetic for the poor water. Nothing was melting now outside. The hand of cold smothered the earth. If we could find one of the old mineshafts then we could maybe climb down inside the mountain, avoiding hours exposed to The Storm. The photograph had featured the old hotel as a backdrop for the miners. A mineshaft was likely to be close, but now buried in an icy grave.

For a moment I thought I'd found the key to the back door under the loose stone that exists for things to be found under and shielded in-between. The stone caught my fingers on the way back down; gap between the stone and its neighbours too small. More of a crack than a gap. It might have been an escape route for water, with its flexibility greater than an Eastern Block gymnast circa 1980s. It might have been an escape route for cavers, the strange breed of anti-mountaineers that crave to be squeezed by rock as others hug the sky, but not for us. The Storm would have to shake my own foundations to shift my dislike of small spaces and passage within. Again, I would keep the information to myself, like the cigarette smoke, now the tunnels too would be demons to hunt me and make me feel ashamed.

"Hundreds died in its construction you know."

I could see Arlanda standing next me as I looked head on into the mirror, although I didn't want to think of him as Arlanda, this man had a sternness akin to a machinist turning the same lathe for thirty years. The little joys that grow like moss for those who appreciate the transportable version of grass had died for him. Only deep concentration remained.

"What do you have for me now? The last time you left blood that saved a life and now?"

"I left no blood. It was there all along and you found it, eventually. You've been back to our world; I told you that you didn't belong. There is no ticket to The Islands for you."

"How did you die?"

The throbbing in my head had returned like a maniac with a staple gun. Computers can get injuries and so when you drag a window, you see beneath to the document before. I based my assumption that the brain had an operating system too and I was seeing the document below the one which should have been drawn on my screen. And so my question was firm and direct and took him by surprise.

"You're the one who is dead, frozen in your tent. I did not die. The Storm chose me and took me straight to The Islands."

"Then why is your body in a hotel room? I haven't seen dead before, but now I can recognise when someone has lost their life."

"I am dead in your world and you are dead in mine, the real world, not as now, when you are dreaming."

"It is in my dreams that I'm in your world. I know when I'm awake..."

"Is that so?" he paused and smiled. The machinist seeing the apprentice tackle the change of the drill bit for the first time.

"Yes so. In my dreams you are waiting like me, waiting to go to The Islands. You weren't chosen and taken straight there on the first flight. You are waiting like me."

"I remember you. I got first class and you got bumped. All a bit hazy now of course, as that was seven years ago. The first day of The Storm was seven years ago today." He leant over and the reflection in the mirror disappeared behind my shoulder. "One more thing you should know... I would never touch the stuff, tobacco, I don't smoke."

Chapter 19

bocata

I think she wanted to be sick more than anything. She made the gasping associated with impending projection, but her body could not expel what was making her sick.

They had been apart for far longer, but that was when she knew he was coming back to her. I tried to think of something that would ease. Words both bind and tear. Silence was my only option, but it was a word in itself as it signalled I was present and the choice had been made to stay there and support her. We sometimes just need to know someone is there, to carry the silence with us. It has a weight, like a sack of letters that someday will be delivered and read.

Should I have told Andrea there and then that Espen was coming back to her? I chose to keep The Islands to myself. People could understand a storm and the need to shelter from it but unless they had experienced my dreams like I had, then they would look at the bruising across my forehead and tell me to get some rest. I didn't like people doing that; making me feel weak. For so long I had felt like I had had the shorter legs, always running to keep up and now I didn't want that to be noticed, for then I would have to admit it to be true also; the possibility that I was mad.

I liked my dreams better. I liked that idea of myself and Espen, warriors, returning to the battlefield from the safety of home, returning on a rescue mission. Maybe my mind was acting out what I wanted to happen so as to make what had, numb to the touch. A nerve that has been bruised is likely to heal. If it was my mind, it would be temporary and real feelings would return; for my anger over losing my friend was being overcome by a sense of purpose. Did I want my anger back? I had never been comfortable with anger. It was like an ocean storm within a swimming pool. Water would splash wildly within something contained. A storm is meant to rip at sea walls and send mighty oaks to the place where they can be young acorns once more in the fields where the lovers met on check blankets; not to just make foam that wilted more rapidly than home-steamed milk.

I carried sadness better. The stillness of a grey Autumn day where everything is not dead. That is sadness to an expert; used to its chilly cloaking air. But if you have always lived upon tropical plains then it is the end of the world where the green of life has become brown and you have forgotten about the existence of Spring.

To have a purpose is to discover Spring; to discover that even when huge branches of growth have died, new growth, new shoots can come from the stem. If you are a true expert at handling sadness it can be turned for good.

Andrea was deep within winter. A winter where the wind had found its opera lungs, instead of the tame melodies of pop. She was trying to shelter from its bitter bite the best she could but there was no shelter from the purest form of sadness; loss. No fire will warm you. No wall will shield you. No candle will hold a flame. The season of loss rages silently along the canals where blood should be.

Still she couldn't be sick. She had flushed the toilet, but there was really no need, it was a pretence; to herself or to me that there was something to flush away. But winter cannot easily find its way out from a maze. It can remain lost for years. And so, that was how I discovered my purpose which brought about the first daffodil and the promise of Easter within my heart and the purpose was to bring about the same feeling in Andrea and Lothen; battling their hurt in their own way. Andrea had let go of any strength. Lothen was trying to provide strength - perhaps imagining some stranger in an airport who gave him a message of hope.

I maybe couldn't reunite love, that was beyond my control and in the hands of the air crew of Welken Airways, but I could reunite the pieces of a broken heart.

Even china can be stuck with glue. Human organs are in no way as brittle as china.

"We are not alone in this hotel Andrea. I smelt cigarette smoke when we first came in. I don't think it was the man we found, he had unfortunately been dead too long. We have to find the smoker."

"Why? Are there not enough mad men already? I'm being told that everything will be alright and that cups of tea will somehow make it go away."

"Because they may have lost someone too and they shouldn't be on their own to feel sick. You are not on your own here. Our pilot lost his wife, Evelyn. She was taken by The Storm too and if so few of us have been affected so much, then many more would have suffered and we need to reach out and help if we can."

Andrea looked up at me, instead of down into the basin.

"Why can't The Storm take me too, to be with Espen again?"

This was the one question I did not want her to ask. I did not have an answer as I didn't know the master of The Storm. Within my dreams The Islands seemed to be a place of goodness, a paradise perhaps, but tearing apart loved ones to inhabit the beaches seemed cruel and there was still the very real possibility that Espen had had a darkness lurking within, something so frightening that he had forgotten about his love for Andrea, he had forgotten about the shade-giving tree they would lie under in the Palace Park in the height of summer when time would pass as slowly as Greek-island time. I didn't know the master of The Storm within Espen. My only answer was a sympathetic shrug. Sympathetic shrugs pass slower than normal and kind of only squeeze, without ever releasing; more of a trapezoid toning than a vowel within body language.

"I'll keep you company, if you must upstairs again and search rooms, but only if you tell me something I've always wanted to know. What did you think of me when Espen first introduced us?"

I'd spent a whole afternoon loading tracks onto my first iPod. Still, I only seemed to have a soundtrack of U2 to take me down Karl Johan and to Bocata Café. I would have preferred something a little more melancholic like Mew or Moby, generally something beginning with M. It was a long walk, giving me time to reflect on how quickly life can change and how slowly it can take to get there. Other friends had met someone and generally that signified toys to be stored away from the main living room for rainy days only. Little spikes of jealousy would rupture my skin but I would push them back inside as I only wanted the best for my friends and they had usually met the best for them.

I knew it must have been Espen that had chosen Bocota as only he would have known I was comfortable there, for one of my bizarre reasons like the width of the room - nice and narrow, somehow folding the light so it made more contrasting shadows; on faces and walls. Shadows were important to me, just like having seats that were square and of equal height to all other seats. Candles as well, if they have the potential to be alight then they must be lit.

When I entered any confined public space, bar, restaurant, café, or shoe shop; I would become Jet Li, just for a moment. No one would see me but somehow I would be making my order with a couple of words before the door had closed. This was my self-defence.

She was called Andrea. Her beauty was genuine - radiating warmth, not freezing water-compounds. Immediately I knew Espen could take her to see his Grandma and Andrea would give her a hug like you give an old teddy a hug that has been in the sock drawer for a year too long. You notice it smells a little odd but you hug it firm and close, without a rush for it to rejoin the sock mutilated by front-line battle in training shoes. I knew she would choose a nice dress too, something with little flowers on cream that would pass admirably next to her bronze nipple-length hair. The greatest shade of blonde is bronze, not tainted by chemicals it shines forth the richness within.

She made a comment about my style. *A typical girl* had passed through my head but it had been intended to show that she noticed the little things that are big on importance to people. Like the design of T-shirt I chose to wear. Both T-shirts and comments about T-shirts speak more than a résumé. Indeed it should be part of any aptitude test for employment but is disregarded as out-of-office attire.

Questions and insight on my appreciation of coffee and the ascent of the mighty true macchiato followed. I liked her. Moreover, I liked that Espen liked her as she seemed someone who would not just be a capacitor, storing up love that was received, but a spring, keeping things in equal tension and quelling vibration. Like a fisherman who does not need to take home the biggest catch as long as some fish go home happy, I was content. I was content that my friend had found something to make the machine of man run smoother and know that it doesn't always need to be running, working hard doing what machines do.

"I don't have a sister, but if I did, only Espen would have been allowed to win her heart. You won Espen's heart and so I love you like a sister," I answered and then we headed down the corridor to the stairs that led to the first floor.

Chapter 20

smoke lingers

Draw a line and people will follow. Build a wall and a line cannot find its path. I didn't know if I wanted to find another hotel guest. If they hadn't sort help then they would not gratefully receive it. The top step of all stairs is where you stop; that is its purpose, re-acclimatising you to the prospect of staying on the same level, of not going up anymore. I stopped for longer than normal. I was drawing a line behind me. A dangerous thing. A thing of great responsibility when people begin following it; for if you can draw a line, you can easily, perhaps accidentally build a wall too.

Right now, Andrea needed Espen more than ever before, just to release the tension in her sails, to bring under control her racing knots. Instead, she had me. I always wanted to get somewhere, or to feel busy that I was on my way.

Andrea needed to rest. I needed to rest, to let cells put up scaffolding and replenish the damaged bricks. But Espen wasn't here to know the force of the wind. He always knew when to sail and then he sailed really hard, but also he knew when to stay in the mooring and let other boats meet the waves. He was very good at taking the time to heal the quickest. He always told me that life takes its toll on us; every day that our body is at work, we build up a debt of a sixth of a day of tiredness and therefore every seventh day we need complete rest and that was the true design behind the week. He would switch off his phone, maybe take to a boat, or a bed, but either way, he lived six days a week with more strength than on my finest ever day, when all cylinders fired as if new and covered in magnetic oil.

This was my seventh day, moreover, I had been on my seventh day for a while now, yet I pushed on. After a pause on the top step I began to walk down to the opposite end of the corridor to the first guest we had found. I was sure that Nielsen would have done the same, that was how he found the body in the first place, searching rooms, but objects can move between rooms. Moving objects can return to a room that has been searched before.

I could smell cigarette smoke. I was particularly sensitive to its odour. If I swallowed sand, that was a similar sensation to smelling smoke to me; very different to cigar smoke. Cigarette smoke had no memory attached, whereas cigar smoke would linger long in the halls of our home and therefore it was a part of home, like the leather and the fireplaces with log ashes within.

"I can smell cigarette smoke."

I looked at Andrea who was stepping ahead, who was beginning to lead and not follow the white line. A leader must always know where the white line is to be drawn or they cannot possibly protect their followers.

"Are we really trying to find someone who needs our help?" she continued, "or do you think there is someone hiding here who might harm us? No one can hurt me more right now, I am not accepting it. Why hasn't anyone come for us? Why can't we raise the alarm and why didn't we search for Espen? We still could. You have seen people on the mountain, coming down right now. They have survived. We could be out there searching, but we are just waiting here, waiting for apparent soldiers of Hell to arrive and then what? This is already hell; they are arriving to fight a battle that has passed this way before them. I say that there are no soldiers of Hell, that it is one of the many climbing parties that had gone out there with us before The Storm, on their way back down and the cigarette smoke is from their friend, waiting outside the door, nervously smoking, willing them to return."

Straight ahead of us was the fire door, built into the hillside, it exited the building onto level ground. Wind had lashed at her sails now and white horses tipped all waves. Andrea was gone, her boat had a destination and she wasn't about to pull back.

I tried to run after her. The Pilot's warning of the nature of the returning storm echoed inside. This storm was not the same, it blew hell ward, it would never take Andrea to where she wanted and so I found another sail of my own and headed through the fire exit as well.

The cold air hit me as only cold air can; creating instant headache pain.

Air is not a loyal subject. It has no master, no king. A terrorist on an unknown side; it will be your perfect neighbour for years, cutting the lawn on every Saturday and going to church on Sunday, always giving at the collection with time to talk to the old over coffee and cinnamon rolls. But one day it will betray you. Today was my day to be surprised.

I gasped for breath as the stealth wind rushed over my mouth, pinning all entrances shut. Unquenched, alveoli cried out for help, but the wind did not hear, or was now not the neighbour I had thought it had been. I had taken three steps. Andrea had taken perhaps eleven steps from the hotel. If she had only taken seven I could have perhaps reached her as I fell to my knees. Finger tips could have taken a hold on the thread of a jumper. All you need is a thread to change someone's mind. The slightest tug in the opposite direction. You do not need to hold tight in a bear hug to show that they are loved still. A bear does not give the most gentle of hugs. The slightest inertia break can change the course of wars.

I reached out into the jet exhaust and could not reach even a thread. Andrea remained too far away for my shouts to carry. My voice was propelled to the sink hole where the wind flowed, brainwashed after its time in camp with all the air in the world. The flow was in the wrong direction.

My eyes closed. I couldn't help it. By instinct they had become mere letterboxes. My body was protecting

93

my portals, my DVD-R drives and USB, without which no information could be received and written to drives. Just in the same way I had made pencil cushions for letters on my page that strayed from the straight line when I learnt to write as a boy. Letters needed protecting when they fell too, I had presumed. Lines could be sharp. Our need to protect is an organ, organ number twenty-four. Like a liver breaks down fat and skin the human bubble wrap for all methods of transportation. The need to protect are the tissues that surround the heart, feeling the thump and tug of its beat endlessly, learning that is a good thing and must be preserved in all hearts as long as possible.

Was my organ of protection damaged, its tissues diseased? For I was seemingly destroying what I was meant to protect. A good friend sees their friend's partner as the same as the friend, chosen to share fungal spores, the organ of protection should secrete hormones when either is drowning in ocean or on land.

But I could not reach her with my fingertips. My arms that were longer than they looked when I looked down at their dinosaur form, bent and awaiting something to hold; were not long enough. And I could not open my eyes. The seal to the flooded chamber on the submarine had been closed and locked off. Tiredness burst forth. Exciting my body like espresso, I didn't even feel myself jump but I knew I was falling.

Arlanda could not stay still. He kept shuffling. There was no other noise in the airport. The conveyor belts did their conveying silently and Frida did her typing using a keyboard with foam keys.

Therefore the shuffling annoyed me. Therefore the shuffling was more evident than during other periods as it was a constant factor, like fridges at night time. Not only the nights are cold. We all shuffle. Fingers. Underpants. Itchy underside of knees. Things just need to rub up against something else from time to time.

And fridges are on, doing the wonder of turning gases from liquid to vapour and heat to cold.

"Please, can you quit that, just quit it..."

"Sorry Nikolai, I just can't help it. I'm getting withdrawal symptoms. There is just no where to buy any here."

"Buy what?"

"Smokes. Cigarettes. Bad habit I know but some people have to have a crossword in the paper to doodle on and I need a cigarette. I hope I can get some in The Islands..."

I turned to look at the check-in desk, now further away than I remembered it. Frida briefly looked up and shook her head.

It could have meant anything. Just like someone saying *see you soon*. That could be tomorrow, or in fact they are bored by you but are chicken to say as they like the free cake.

It could have just been a stiff neck. It could have been no ticket for The Islands available yet, or that The Islands was a smoke free zone. I trusted that whatever she meant by it, the reasons were noble. The airport was a place of safety, a tranquil place I had found to shelter from The Storm. I trusted Frida and Arlanda totally.

The shuffling now bothered me less. I could live with it. I could even live with the fact that Arlanda had to smoke and maybe would cough and slow us down if we ever climbed a mountain together, but I couldn't live with myself for believing the man who I had seen in the basement and in the bathroom. He was from somewhere deep in my archive of movies that had scared me a little too much to look in the mirror afterwards. He wasn't Arlanda. He didn't make me feel safe and he wasn't to be trusted. There wasn't anyone else in the hotel. I had led Andrea up the stairs and to her escape because of my belief in there being other survivors in the hotel. She had found an exit because of me. She wasn't supposed to go into The Storm. She could never find her way back to Espen by walking alone.

I gasped. The air apologised for its behaviour and filled my lungs. The wind had dropped without a parachute and the tears from heaven had stopped.

In front of me I could see the deep channels carved by Andrea's leg and hip motion. But she was no longer within eleven strides. She was further away than the light of the hotel permitted me to see.

The darkness in front of my eyes acted as a blank canvas for art to begin. The torch light was now close. They were over the last ridge and on the final path. The final path was not long. I could run it in five minutes if I was hungry and knew there was someone waiting to feed me.

Andrea had run towards the people descending the mountain and they were coming to us with purpose and haste.

Chapter 21

X and Y

There was no doubt, sunny days were the best. Days when blue was the only colour of the sky. I loved the energy of clouds, crossing continents, crossing borders without ever stopping. I loved days when the clouds said hello and touched the ground, but no day, such as a sunny day, gave me the same euphoric feeling. A little sunshine and I was on a beach in Portugal running through the cave to the secret cove before the tide filled the entrance, looking for my green ball which seemed to want to make a break for Africa. Or, I was in the square in Sienna looking for a place to sit down and have a Coke, shielded from the sun's brashness by sunglasses as if the helmet of a space-walking astronaut. Sunshine evacuated all that blocked the flow of happiness in my body.

But I had long wondered about the days when the sky is criss-crossed by a myriad of cloud formations, all bubbling away like chemistry. Most days like this, the sunshine comes, and it goes. What is evacuated returns and blocks your passages to freedom. It is inevitable that a cloud will stray in front of the sun at some point, but what if they never do, that by some freak chance the sun always finds a path down to the earth where you are, in-between the clouds? Like a bird dodging the traffic on the highway.

Did such days exist? Was the sunshine of equal value even though you had failed to believe in it as much?

I had to find Andrea. It was my fault she had got the notion in her belly to leave the hotel and perhaps search the mountain herself. I should have just let her be sick in that bathroom, given her the time for saliva to run wild and temperature to soar before the bodily convulsion; that for a brief second makes you give up your hold on everything. But no, I had longed to show her to her garden patch where she could grow Spring.

I was letting heavy clouds in all around, into my thoughts and actions. Would the sunshine still find its path I wondered? Would I know what to do to save us, to bring us down the mountain and lead Lothen to Evelyn and Andrea to peace?

The lights coming down the mountain had stopped jiggling around like sparklers from a hundred metres.

Either they had stopped to tie a shoe, to ready their arms, or Andrea had caught them up. Minutes passed and the lights were dimmed, pointing down at the ground while a conversation was had.

Perhaps I wasn't supposed to do it on my own. Perhaps these men were men forged from the finest X and Y chromosomes and would lead us down the mountain, by tunnel or lull in The Storm. I longed for that, to not be the only one responsible to pass on knowledge of how to get seeds to grow when all you have is hard soil, for my soil only supported the nettles and grass that would grow unplanted.

I forced every step, almost swimming in the snow and made my way from the hotel, my beach, my place where my sand castle was, and out into the ocean where I could hardly see the beach anymore.

I felt the cold biting at me like a thousand soldier ants. It must have been midnight. I had lost the thread of time. It now span across the globe without me holding on. We had left the hotel on the Friday morning. A plethora of woollen garments had sunned themselves under the long porch as we started our trail north. For two nights we had shivered in the first storm, trapped by its fierce argument with the granite. So, this was the third night. That was what it should have been, but then I should have been cleaning my teeth about now in front of my bathroom mirror half the size of the wall, which still somehow neglected to show-up every blemish before I stepped outside into the blemish-free-zone. I should have been soaking up the last glimpses of the weekend in my magazine cutting from an IKEA magazine. Vivid colour and pine. My home to me was what an aircraft hanger was to a plane. Pressures were checked, oils replenished and engines examined for metal fatigue. Without the time in the hanger, my parts were weary of all the travelling, all the take-offs and landing. It should have been the third night, but it felt like many more. I could feel it in my feet, the black box flight recorders of human flight. Could it have been seven years as my vision in the bathroom had suggested? Was he just projecting my deepest fears? I knew I was rapidly ageing. As if I was on a canyon of rapids in a dingy, I was hopelessly sticking out my paddle to try to stop in the fastest flow of the river. I was a few years into the post-twenty-five canyon and it scared me that it only ever flowed quicker. So perhaps it had only been three nights and my fourth could be spent back in the familiarity of Oslo, where I knew the canyon waters flowed quickly but not out of control.

Paths find their way by cutting a groove; therefore humans can follow and keep it worn. I could see the hollows in the snow under the slightest hint of moon. And there were the rocks still protruding from their woolly jacket, marked by red .paint, telling me the way of the path through the foothills and eventually to the summit ridge.

Plus there were Andrea's footprints of course. They were deep but compacted which meant I surged quickly up the mountain, almost having a staircase to climb. Ricocheting in my mind were the angry words of Lothen, The Pilot, who would surely be cursing me for stepping out into The Storm he warned of. Maybe he would look upon me as tainted now, maybe he would not allow me back into the hotel and I would be quarantined outside.

Acceptance was what I craved. That was what pushed every beat in my chest forward with might. I did not want cursed words from Lothen and for him to think that I was not capable of holding my promise of finding Evelyn, even though I didn't think I had made such a promise. If we had actually been on the mountain for seven years, I might have had time to travel to The Islands and return, having met his Evelyn, but it was a weight to need to fulfil a promise which was potentially impossible, moreover, lunacy. I also needed Nielsen to look upon me as an equal man, someone who could chop down the same size tree and not letting Andrea face the newcomers alone, or disappear in search of Espen never to be seen again, was a certain way to at least show I was capable of yielding an axe if the duty called.

No doubt they could hear me before I could see their torch light. My breathing was strained, not severely, but enough to not be marine-silent. They would have had time to make assessments, to fully glue their cover and poke a weapon in Andrea's back.

I saw her first and the first thing I noticed was the colour. There was colour in her cheeks, the like of which I had not seen since the first climb. She looked healthy and not sick anymore.

There were four of them. I made a snap judgement that they were all men but the fourth was in so much shadow that they could have been a woman, or a beast. They wore military attire, Air Force suits and mountain boots. The colours were charcoal and not luminous orange. They had small backpacks and I could see ribbons of parachute poking out and their flight helmets were also strapped to their backs.

"They are here to save us. Norwegian Air Force. Their planes went down in the storm and they will lead us all down the mountain and rescue by their squadron. They have already been in contact with their superiors down in Fortun where the other hotel guests and climbers are sheltering. Helicopters are on their way. At first light they will sweep the mountain in search of Espen. They have survived up there without tents for two days in a snow hole, Espen could have as well...He knew how to dig a snow hole," declared Andrea, well into the valley of hope, unable to see the climb ahead that might have just been too steep to pass.

I looked at the four pilots. Stern faces greeted me, looks that had a precise purpose with no room for jollity.

"Which one are you?" asked the pilot I could see most clearly. For a moment I was sure he looked identical to the maths teacher who had subtracted much from my learning and added nothing. For a moment he was a demon from my early years, someone who had made me feel I was not up to the grade and once I had felt that, I had lost my footing on the giant conveyor belt of passage to getting a delivery stamp and progressing to my final destination. The moment passed. I looked closer and he actually had a thick beard and was far too tall. My maths teacher had been neither bearded nor a colossus. In fact I doubted he could have saved me from drowning if I had fallen into a swimming pool still with the cover on, but this man could. His shoulders were as wide as I felt I was tall.

"Nikolai," I answered, not knowing if the demons were within me or in front of me.

"Nikolai. Are you sure?"

"What do you mean?"

"You are not on our list."

There was a piece of paper in his hands with pencil scribbles on, folded many times and not in a planned way like origami.

"What list?"

"The list of survivors."

Chapter 22

boarding card

"Are you angry with me Nikolai for leaving the hotel?"

I was last in the line of six making the final short journey back to the hotel that glowed in the foreground. The air crew had immediately started their march again once they had attained my name. They had not explained what the list was, where it came from or what it meant for those on it, or not on it.

"I'm angry with myself for leading you on a search of the hotel and not letting you rest. So, no, I'm not angry with you. I understand that you have to find your own conclusion, that it is your right as Espen's love, to love him, yearn for him and search for him until the very end. But the helicopter pilot, Lothen, won't be happy. He instructed us to stay indoors and he feared what was out there...including these pilots."

Andrea stopped and turned around abruptly.

"You think the helicopter pilot said all this?"

"Yes of course, he barricaded the hotel doors when he came back around..."

"That was you, Nikolai, you stood guard at the front door and told us about these crazy notions that the storm was now blowing hell ward and the soldiers of hell were descending the mountain. This was all you. And you kept mentioning an Evelyn. Who is she? I know your life intimately and you don't know anyone called Evelyn."

"That, that is impossible, it was him, Lothen, he woke up and did all this..."

"He is dead. We never found the blood plasma, you never found it. He bled to death on the kitchen work tops."

I stumbled and as I crouched I could see my sleeves. An iridescent orange. An orange that is a warning to all shepherds.

"I saw him. I heard his voice. He told me his name," I said to myself, picturing every scene. It was then I really noticed the pain in my head. I had forgotten about it for a while. I lifted my hand and I could feel the warmth emitted by the blood before I even touched it. Just how badly injured was I? Was I even awake? I had never seen Lothen together with the others. I had spoken to him alone. But I didn't remember saying his words, pretending to be him. That was not the version of history recorded within me.

Helicopter crashes are not the easiest to survive. They fall and never glide to impact. Maybe I never made it, maybe none of us did. That day could have been our time to go. But no one was at rest. We were all still searching. If it had been my time, I would have hoped to find rest.

Nielsen needed answers.

Sara needed for everyone to be well.

Andrea needed to find Espen.

Espen was lost.

Lothen needed a promise fulfilled.

I had to keep a promise.

As the intense cold of sitting on the snow encroached upward through my nether regions, I decided that things were only real to you, privately. What you felt to be real, events and senses were all relative. A man lying in a coma in a dream world might never know he is in a coma if he never wakes up to be told, therefore to him, everything he experiences is his reality until otherwise re-orientated and he has to make his decisions based on that reality and the morality that exists there.

Therefore, we had been stranded two nights in our tent before rescue this morning. The helicopter had crashed but we all survived. I found the blood plasma in the basement emergency supplies and the helicopter pilot eventually regained consciousness to tell tales of where he had been, perhaps the same dream world as me, the place on the edge of life due to our severe injuries. This was the reality I would base my decisions on. In this reality, Lothen had not died and he was the one who had barricaded us in the hotel and warned of the new storm. This meant Andrea was lying; forced to by the newcomers who were what Lothen had said they were; our inner demons, the soldiers of hell.

I had to stop them. I had to warn the others at the hotel that the Norwegian Air Force hadn't bailed out over the mountains and were not our rescue team.

My mind knew its task, but my body did not. My legs did not respond to polite English gestures to stand up. Even when I got a bit hot, frothy and Hispanic on my reflexes, there was no response. As my head nestled into a snow pillow, I knew I was leaving behind a pink Slush Puppy. This end would befit me better than a sudden crash. A slip rather than a slide.

Nielsen would protect them. He was a bit of an idiot at times, thinking he was just that little bit better, better at climbing, better looking, better at winning the opposite sex. But his heart grew the Norwegian way. Slowly it lay down its rings, making it extremely strong and durable. He would see through the apparent rescuers. He would protect my closest friends.

My arm was tugged repeatedly. I blinked and recognised the light to be intensely white and pure. I was in the airport again and Arlanda was stood up from where we had been sat down and was pulling at my clothing, with urgency.

"What is it?"

"We're off Nikolai. Our plane is ready for boarding at gate seven. Frida has called us, the last call."

"I don't have a ticket. I haven't completed my tasks...anywhere near to completing my tasks."

Arlanda smiled. I could see that genuine joy creased his shiny skin.

"Yes you do. We're both going to The Islands and we are going now."

Chapter 23

frida

I couldn't recall the first flight I took, but I remembered the destination. My first really hot place and the first place where pebbles had become sand to be used in the arts and crafts corner; moulded and shaped with the help of a little water - the miracle substance that can both bind and wash away.

Phases of life had coincided with air travel. There was a time when I didn't even think about the plane journey and I didn't really need to think about any practical aspect of life either. Life was a thing of play. That period lasted the longest but very suddenly dawned into a new day where I was worried about every nut and bolt, the wings and most of all the precious engines; willing them to keep their propulsion up, to keep the turbines turning and chucking in that fuel to be burnt to keep the laws of physics from being angry. During this time, everything in life was a worry as the first rays of responsibility caught my eyes from the beautiful dawn. Now I was used to the responsibility. I had come to terms with the fact that the bell had rung on playtime and I was not in the lesson learning anymore, making sketches of how a U-shaped valley was formed. This phase meant you had to pass it on, to stand in front of people and convince them you had the lights switched on and knew what you were talking about.

So, I was used to managing my land-based ship and didn't have to think about air-born transit. Things had come full circle.

My mind was full of just a bit of bric-a-brac as Frida handed me a boarding card for Island Nine, Flight Seven, Welken Airways. But it suddenly hit me that I hadn't earned the boarding card. I had done nothing to protect nor further the rescue of my friends. My bric-a-brac turned into oak tables and wardrobes. Heavy and cumbersome, my thoughts weighed on my steps forward.

"Why do I have a boarding card, I didn't complete my task?"

"What task?"

"To lead my friends down the mountain and to safety..."

"But that is what you did. By being a friend, by caring for them; carrying their troubles as if they were your own. People are designed to not be strong enough on their own. You didn't know this and yet you interlocked your fingers and carried their weights. We are therefore honoured to have you on board Nikolai. Everyone at The Islands shares this urge to carry other's luggage, even if they cannot pick it up or find its rightful place. No one is perfect on The Islands. There are few heroes but many heroic hearts.

"I haven't actually saved them though, Andrea is in the company of the enemy, men who are making lists of survivors and seemingly surviving fine themselves. Sara is living with not being able to save lives, her grandma, the hotel guest, and apparently The Pilot. I don't know how much more capacity she has. And Nielsen, he is like a captive elephant, he needs to lead the family across the plains and yet he is caged in. They are not in a safe place. The soldiers of hell are coming, or have arrived..."

"You cannot get to The Islands from your actions. Actions do not matter. The call of your heart is what matters. You are now talking about a place you have left. Our skies are blue and snow free. Welken Airways operate one way only. So, you can go back to the mountain and face the trials or you can come with us on the last flight. We have a seat for you."

"My friends should be coming too. I am no more worthy. I haven't saved lives or made life full of laughter. They should at least be here."

"Maybe they have already travelled and are waiting for you. It is their decision to travel or not, you cannot carry everything."

Arlanda suddenly re-appeared in the passageway towards the departure gate. He raised his eyebrows, the time-honoured way to speed people up, be it with dinner or post office queues.

"What's the hold-up Nikolai? You have to come with me. There are mountains there for us to climb, and I cannot find my wife on my own, I need your help. She has travelled on ahead and there are many islands to search."

"What is the decision Nikolai? I cannot hold your boarding pass for much longer."

"OK, I will go and help Arlanda."

"You promise?" he asked, anxiously ruffling hair that was no longer there, just the ghost of what could be ruffled.

"I promise to help you find her."

I collected my pass from Frida who promptly closed the gate. It was then I could see a few other people arriving in the airport, beginning their aimless wander around, slowly building up the courage to talk to or continue to ignore each other. I couldn't help them now. My seat beckoned. I was suddenly tired of wanting to fix the troubles of an army and only having brittle Cellotape to do it. Cellotape was not enough. It was temporary. Its glue would at some time become dry and curtains were way beyond its fixing ability, even when combined with the might of blue-tack. I knew that now.

I followed Arlanda through security. I was travelling light. Years ago I would have had a teddy bear in tow at the very least and perhaps several family members carrying a fluffy friend as well.

A boy had become a man but the teddy bear had stayed young and slowly was left at home to wonder how it was outside now, haunted by the bad memories of x-ray machines and the threat of the drugs search to a teddy bear; gutting by knife, if it travelled with an adult.

I caught up Arlanda and my questions tried to catch up with my mind.

"You lost your wife in The Storm as well?" I asked, thinking about The Pilot and all the promises I had been making, willy-nilly, as if I was throwing up dollars into the air.

"As I said, I woke to find the front door open and just footprints into the snow that slowly engulfed them. She had gone. I ate breakfast alone for the first time in many years that morning. She was never a big fan of breakfast. An apple maybe or the ubiquitous slice of bread and perennial jam, but her nutrition didn't come from the food and neither did mine, I discovered. I searched the mountains for her and all I found was you and your friends and now all I have left is you."

"You're Lothen?"

"Lothen Arlanda, but people call me Arlanda, as I introduced myself to you. Did I introduce myself as something else in the helicopter? Didn't you know that I am your helicopter pilot? Maybe I shouldn't have reminded you as I crashed after all...I guess you never saw me close-up, just the back of my head, or should I say helmet."

He was right. I hadn't seen his face when in the helicopter and afterwards it had been covered in blood. Sara had tended to him most. I had been on a mission to find blood plasma.

I was disappointed.

I had thought that I had saved The Pilot, after having found the blood plasma in the basement, but the timeline thread I had followed all my life had now become frayed; dancing threads into the air that I couldn't gather together into one strong cord. He mustn't have made it, Arlanda, as he was here, travelling with me to The Islands.

I was disappointed.

I mustn't have made it either, or had drifted in and out of deep unconsciousness. It appeared a helicopter crash was the end that befitted me, had been chosen to fit my feet.

The first rays of dawn met my eyes. I was awake now. I was awake now, not the other way round. The Lothen I had spoken to in the hotel reminded me very much an actor I had seen in a film, invisible to bullets but imprinted on my mind. And then the hotel, I had maybe dreamt about a hotel in the mountains, I wasn't even sure if we'd ever stayed there, it was somewhere I had always wanted to stay.

"And your wife's name?"

"I've told you, I've told you all about her and her heart of only goodness, my Evelyn."

Chapter 24

one-way

I always try to check the engines. Now, I know nothing about jet engines apart from something that I heard or read but and I am not a qualified authority to repeat it successfully. My comprehension was that the fuel was only burnt to keep the old man of physics happy that the equations of energy were in the wondrous zone of equilibrium.

My theory was, why use fuel? It's expensive and harmful. One could just use a substitute, a dummy fuel. The old man of physics would never know. But yet with such basic knowledge, I would always glance right when boarding a plane, through the little window in the gantry and check the turbine blades. Not for metal fatigue or bird strike damage, but for shininess. If something looks nice then it is less likely to kill you.

There was no view, no window out onto the runway, to be able to see what was to come or what was going to take me there. Like every plane journey as an adult, I would have to get over the step of control. On one side was where I wished to have the controls; to steer and to fold the map where it was never designed to fold flush. On the other side of the step was where everything was carried out unseen and by unseen hands and I just had to trust that they were holding the map the right way up and knew left from right. It was a difficult step to take even on a calm day when holidays awaited. Days of disconnection. Days of discovery of how slowly time can actually pass if you remove the engines. Often the step would be forced upon you, a nudge from an air stewardess in the form of direction to your seat. Once strapped in, you are the other side of the step if you like it or not. Today was different, I had not chosen to travel, but been chosen. The destination sounded idyllic, but I was not ready to just abandon my unfinished painting. Yes, I had struggled to paint. I wasn't gifted with brush-strokes or an eye for colour but parts had taken shape and much had been sketched in to finish at a later date. Just like leaving a plate of food that I could have eaten due to young after burners of metabolism, I needed to leave more than a sketch. I needed to save my friends from the vicious mountain and I needed to see my city again.

"One-way," I whispered to myself, "Is the longest way."

When teams were picked at school, the strict etiquette of popularity and girl-pulling power was followed. I could run. I could run as fast as the inland breeze. But I wasn't an ocean storm. A hurricane, propelling all into its centre. I was nervous about what life was in waiting; the skills I would need to not be picked last for team events, destined to keep goal badly. I was nervous about things that had never before scratched at my nerves. What if I couldn't find my seat? What if I didn't know how to use the seatbelt? What if for an unexplained reason, I did not fit, that the seat was too big or too small to be comfortable for the duration of the flight? And the food, it worried me the most. If it would be rice, or pasta, potatoes or wheat, my stomach needed time to ready its army, form a defensive line and halt the Viking invasion before York.

I was sensitive to all things new. That included destinations, people and dreams. My dreams had long concerned me. Most dreams have an air of familiarity, like a place you have been to many years before, too many to know the names but you recognise elements and scents over details. But my dreams had been following new scripts, re-writes yet unaired to the screen. The hotel. The airport. My life. One of the three was the dream, or one of the three was real. I had taken for granted that what I had experienced was the straight thread of time, rolling away in the mill, but the hotel and the airport had felt equal to me in terms of sensations. That was where they differed from the script of other dreams; where people you know say and do the most unlikely of things and when you meet them again, a tiny bit of you are still unsure if they actually did, if the prude was the raging addict in hiding.

I could have been in a helicopter crash years earlier, appearing now and again in my new consciousness, or that close miss on the E6 motorway where the car just tucked in within the vacuum of one tick of time to impact, didn't clear the vacuum and struck me head on, sending my torso into the crusher.

None of it could have actually happened - the day I dozed for hours in afternoon sunshine in the Andes, the day a female runner pulled down her shorts and did a pee in the woods as I unexpectedly ran past, the day I got the stone to jump twelve times into the air across the river, the day I only read a book, a good book. None of it could have actually happened. I could be waiting to wake up.

Maybe I had just woken up.

The lights in the cabin dimmed. I was at unease and a coffee would not fix it.

"Just relax. It is a short flight. Routine. You have nothing to worry about."

Frida was one of the flight team. Her words were all carefully chosen; I recognised that for what it was. Kindly meant, meant to settle but not to solve. Only the truth solves, makes the equation in equilibrium and the old man of physics happy. And it wasn't a short flight. That was a lie. One-way lasts forever. It is a very long way to go as you cannot go back.

"I need to know where we are going and why, what my purpose is there, my job and why I have to leave what I have known all these years, I am not ready to leave. I have not loved enough. I have not made enough dinners for others or driven them enough places in a hurry, or built enough sand castles just for children to enjoy seeing them reclaimed by the sea. I need to go back and do all these things and have the anguish of how hard it is to succeed in the simple things. I need to show my friends love, to not let our mountain trip end in disaster..."

Frida leant over. Her teeth were perfect. The way they slid into her gums like a river flows over its bank showed she had been born that way. Her blocks fitted, all geometry had been measured by a master of pencil and set-square.

"You are here because you have followed the white horse. A white horse is a goal formed by love, like the ocean wind that only wants to build up the waves to be higher. Love is the one thing that is tough enough to withstand all. No man-made force can corrupt it, love endures all. Faith on the other hand is a weaker force; it waxes and wanes, wears and tears. Right now, your Faith is tearing and if it tears too much you will keep going back to the place you think of being alive; this hotel in the mountains, or your flat in Oslo, that is when your Faith is having a nervous breakdown, putting you in situations where you feel inadequate and unloved and with the potential to hurt and be hurt. What are The Islands and what do you do there? The Islands are everyone's true home and your only purpose there is to be fulfilled, to be full where you have previously felt empty. Both love and Faith endures on The Islands...but do not question where they are on the map of the world too much, else you may go to sleep again and have nightmares of a hotel where soldiers have arrived to kill you..."

Her gentle tones and gentle caresses imagined from just her eyelash flickers were sharpened on a stone harder than a knife blade.

The aircraft cabin became my prison cell. And its pressure the guilt of leaving my friends behind. Perhaps they had faced a similar position to me when the helicopter crashed or The Storm struck the tent. I only took it as given from what my eyes had told me that they had all escaped unscathed. We could have all died, our bubble wrap terminally popped so that it cannot make another delivery. They could have all travelled to The Islands alone and sat in the same seat as I, racked with the pressure of leaving behind the people they loved.

I had no choice but to take the flight. I did not know whether we were unlocking the vault to the Kingdom or whether the soldiers of hell liked the sunshine and you would only know that when you had run out of sunscreen.

Arlanda was rubbing his thumb against his index finger. He needed a reassuring touch or to give reassurance to his wife. By association, she was now part of my guilt-packet, which needed my protection.

"Did you believe in heaven?" I asked.

"Not really," he said with a fading tone. The end of his sentence imagining the alternative to heaven, a place we were living in now or a place we might just have been travelling to.

Chapter 25

butterflies

I rolled over again and nearly dived head first back into the lagoon; the lagoon of deepest sleep where the waters are deep and blue and full of fish that can provide a whole meal. I had lived so many years, just getting by on sleep, setting the alarm an hour earlier than it took to defragment my hard-drive. As a result, I was defragmented on the inside, where my sleep lagoon only harboured small fish; that lived their whole lives to provide someone with half a meal.

Eventually I rolled over enough times that I was on the floor. The sand of the beach filled the cracks in wooden floorboards and dusted the plains in-between the rivulets that fed my lagoon. As I felt the sand begin to stick to a cheek, I knew it was time for maybe another swim in the surf where I floated as if my bones were now made of magnesium. I had never been a great swimmer, but now the sea was my occupation and the beach my recuperation.

This was life on The Islands; where it never got dark and sky always sapphire blue.

In the beach hut with a roof with gaps to the stars I could never see in the daylight and rain would have filtered through except it never rained, I had been dreaming like a small boy again, full of purity and shear acceptance of happiness being our control state of being. It had felt like days since the plane journey and all I could really remember were two things; we were still to find Evelyn and my last dream. I had been dreaming of butterflies, seasons of butterflies.

A butterfly I had once glanced upon in a summer's garden at the break of night fall. The last bronze strips of sunlight reflected on its beautiful wings and then it was gone, up into the sky like embers rising from fire. I longed to maybe see the butterfly again. The next summer came in a moment. I sat and waited but the bronze strips of sunlight were hidden by rain clouds keeping the fragile butterfly away. And a summer turned into two and into three. I had never forgotten the moment I had first glanced upon the butterfly. But life had taken over. I could not always be thinking of the butterfly looping up to the heavens. One day, one mundane and nothing-out-of-the-ordinary day, there it would be, I had told myself. The butterfly again. There would always be another brief chance to glimpse it, but it wouldn't be the exact same butterfly, over time it would have died and given birth to new butterflies that would have continued its first journey. The same pattern on the wings would remain, although the light might have been sepia or scarlet and time might have become the enemy, for both of us.

In my dream I sat at the bottom of the garden every summer's night where the temperature was dipping to the point where a jumper was as welcome as a cool drink had been during the day.

On the beach, I sat and waited, not needing a jumper in the constant twenty-four degrees; enough to make the slightest forehead sweat which leaped into the sea breeze to be carried to the place where clouds learn to float.

But I was a little thirsty. Arlanda would usually bring me a drink from the fountain by our hut and say we should find the boat that travelled between the islands and begin our quest to reunite him and Evelyn. And then he would sleep and maybe dream of her; his summer butterfly that had come back to him, married him and now could have damaged wings that could not carry her to him again as he waited once more on the log in the summer garden he had known well as they dated.

Who was my butterfly? Who had I let stretch beautiful wings and go in search of a different colour sky?

Natalie. Maybe. The butterfly could have been the Czech girl who gave me free coffee as I began to become addicted to coffee. She had gone home and I had to pay for coffee again. But I didn't want there to be two butterflies that could always land at the same time, so I chose the stripes of Natalie at that time; if only to see her hand writing again - the hand writing of an innocent child and grand artist.

Around the corner to the bay we had first walked up from the airstrip, I could see a dark shape bobbing on the waves. I turned away thinking it was seaweed, the loneliest of all plants.

But it was a swimmer. I knew this as they took from swimming the waves and swam their ankles in the coca-cola water bubbling onto the sand.

In this dream I am waiting to see the butterfly again. Any day now, I tell myself, any day now, its wings of destiny will give flight to my life, will move the solid ground.

She walked up the beach yet remained looking out to sea. Maybe for her butterfly or not to disturb the delicate wings of the butterfly she could see sitting on the beach.

She stopped as rigid as a tree.

"Hello," she said and smiled, and the bronze sunlight of a summer's evening was replenished into the midday haze where you can only squint at its splendour.

"You haven't travelled on to the main island yet?" she continued, in an accent akin to the song of the swallow that only appears in mid-summer, the season of greatest growth and rest.

"We've only just arrived, on the last flight from Norway. Frida told us to rest and then we would be summoned onward."

"Funny, Frida told me the same and now I am well rested, in fact I think I could exert myself in one way or another now."

She tilted her head slightly and the sun put gloss on the freckles that passed as galaxies beneath her eyes.

"We could just all go on together."

"We have to find Evelyn."

I pointed at Arlanda; finding new gaps to bridge between sleep and wakefulness as sand flowed ocean-ward from the valley of his knuckles.

"His wife, they've been separated," I added.

"And who do you have to find?"

She turned away as she said it, brushing the air with her outstretched arms as if a ball gown twirled in her wake.

"You," I wanted to say. I wanted to run into the knee deep water and make a second wave to the surf.

Chapter 26

I never ran into the surf. The sand sprinkled across my feet remained dry. Sat in that summer garden on the log, there were times I maybe glimpsed the butterfly again, but with different patterns on the wings I hadn't recognised it, or I had liked the previous pattern best.

The butterfly had become bored that their summer clothing did not catch my gaze. But I had been comfortable just waiting on the log that had seen many before me and would not move, not even for other trees.

In the geography class, we were meant to be learning about where Switzerland was, but Natalie had been more interested in finding out where my feet were. At first I had thought that the rabbit had escaped, had gone in search of burrows without walls. By the time I had realised that it was Natalie and that Switzerland was land-locked, she had stopped and never did it again. I became land-locked, forever trying to find my path to the sea, her open sea, but I had let her fragile wings take flight from my cupped hands.

She was called Ida, and from the way she spent ninety percent of her outward transmission looking across the ocean that only reflected the sun and no other interesting land fall; she was desperate to leave.

Whereas I had been content.

Someone else's restlessness brushed away my ease. She gazed out at the ocean because what she wanted to look at was not on the island she was. Her family, her friends, her summer bird of love, was someplace else, just like Evelyn. I became the man with the map. I became the driver looking for the refuelling stop.

It was time to leave our first taste of paradise, for it too was now feeling like a prison, where the ones you love cannot visit you and spend time with you. Paradise had been an illusion. It had been a stepping stone of rest for paradise is only real when shared.

The man ship wrecked on a desert island of honeymoon bliss, left to eat fish eyes for joy, does not think he is in paradise, but in hell, and the only difference between his perception of paradise and hell, would be one person who he would imagine in his goldfish bowl when looking out across the ocean they were separated by.

"On our first date, I kept her waiting forty-five minutes, maybe more. She had made a latte last for longer than any other customer in history."

"She will be waiting still," I told Arlanda.

He smiled but held back from bursting forth into a grin. She had been the one who had left him after all. Evelyn had chosen to leave her husband's side and be taken by The Storm still wearing her night attire. Or that was his side of the story. Just like my side was that Espen had chosen to leave our mountain adventure when we had needed to stay together the most. That was my side of it. Always easier to leave than be left behind say the ones who didn't carry the burden of luggage. But one-way is the hardest and longest of ways and the ticket not easily purchased. Something stronger had called both Evelyn and Espen and was calling them still.

Ida waved from down the beach. It was not a hello-wave which is as fast as a spinning propeller; neither was it as slow and high as the goodbye-wave which is more like someone reaching for a high shelf. Her gesture pulled at our atoms. Had she seen a boat? Did she have a boat? Was she the one sent to summon us?

The long beach was shorter when walked by two. We had no luggage to carry, only the wind nipped at our yellow shorts to hold us back. I could remember wearing a similar pair back in Oslo, in the city that froze in the winter and breathed in the summer. I could picture one day on a rocky beach; re-colouring my pastel shades. If I could have chosen to bring anything with me, those shorts would not have made the list. They were worn and had been far too many places they shouldn't, yet they had been welcomed into The Islands.

"You boys take the slow lane? Did I not wave wildly enough for you? Tut, if we are to find Evelyn before she is out of reach or out of love then we have to get going."

I liked she used the word tut, not the sound. The sound alone can show irritation and irritate, but she was full of coyness; sweet and sour. I let her wander from flower to flower in her field. By the way her right foot curled over her left and then slid forwards along the timbers of the jetty, she was on a journey of her own; she was trying to find her connection too. In the garden you must leave well alone two butterflies whose tentacles are exploring each other, or the chrysalis that has yet to be transformed. Everything must be given a fair chance. Only when the season has well passed and the chrysalis is hard can you hold out your sugar-palm.

But I couldn't help liking her a little bit, wondering if she painted or gave old people long hugs. And I could look forward to sitting next to her on the boat, that would not disturb metamorphosis; the stages of love.

The boat had at one time been blue. It was no longer vibrant or smooth across its panels, but floated all the same. A man was lying in the shade of his newspaper upturned over his chest. I thought he was asleep but the slight glisten of tears gave away his open eyes.

"Come," he croaked, gesturing more into the air than to us. He was old, as old as his boat. "You kids needing a ride?"

"Yes, but we were told to wait here, you sure you're OK to take us?" I asked. I had expected a yacht with a crew in uniform; uniformed like on Welken Airways.

"There is no waiting on these waters; we're free to go where we please."

His hand waved across the unbroken expanse of ocean.

"We have no money to pay you..."

"Newcomers...always try to pay. Your journey has been paid for already young Sir; the price has already been paid."

I didn't quite understand, not then, not while I was concerned about not looking at Ida's black two piece. I had to look at her feet when I followed and her blue eyes when we spoke, I instructed myself. Easy to let the wild bear encroach on the settlement, a challenge to always keep it to roaming the woods. But the woods were the only place for the wild bear to live; for a bear is only a hunter and love cannot be hunted. It is not a salmon that can be plucked from the Alaskan high river. If love was to come my way, then it would be a delicate butterfly safe in the meadow away from the sleeping bear. My hand would be held out, also a safe place to sun wings you cannot touch.

The engine started as we tried to find the comfortable spot on the plank-seat. There would be a comfortable spot we were all thinking, moving around as if we were rubbing in a cream against soreness. I found a more comfortable spot closer to Ida. I was cushioned by her cushion but I moved away and remained with the feeling of a rat sized mosquito taking a bite as the pressure of the hardwood built up.

The outboard motor found its legs, like a cyclist in the Tour de France who has seen a few too many tours and is facing Mont Ventoux for the last time; lagging behind to begin with but old muscle fibres pulled and pushed and generated a cadence younger engines would have been envious of.

Both wind and salt spray combed my hair with an ever larger comb. I was fourteen again. Responsibility free. Guilt free of responsibilities I hadn't met. It could have been joy. It was a new taste. The drink of choice had always been coffee, so hard to make well and usually bitter on both the melancholic and cup. This was a strawberry milkshake. Not just of the ordinary, but from the quayside in Fredrikstad, in summer, after a wedding, or during, during the bit where one ceremony ends and another tradition begins.

We would find Evelyn. Her arms would take their place on her husband's neck as if a tie to his collar and all would be right with the world.

We would find Espen. His smile would dry all rain soaked ground and signal in the right weather for any adventure and all would be right with the world.

We would find Ida's love. He would be handsome no doubt, both bearded and cut clean. A conqueror of mountains and the cookbook. A man of long phone calls and handy with a hammer.

"Who is he?" I asked. He might have been able to teach me to fish or even dance if we both agreed to not talk about it afterwards or tell anyone.

"Who?"

"The one we need to find for you..."

"Oh, right, I'm still looking. I travel alone. I only went out in The Storm to clear the path. My little apartment gets so snowed in with its basement entrance you know."

"The Storm didn't choose me. I lived through it and was rescued by helicopter and maybe died when it crashed or when I passed out on the mountain trail...But it didn't choose me, I nearly didn't make it here, The Islands, wherever and whenever they are..."

"Nikolai, I didn't die in The Storm. I am alive now and so are you; you are not dead in whatever way you imagine. That is just your doubt, your inner dark doubt trying to hold you back. I'm sure you were chosen too."

"Espen left me. He was chosen. I had to battle against every demon on my own and they rose up in numbers."

I could taste the salt and I could feel the joy curdling. Ida pushed her knee against mine. Innocent knees.

"However you got here, you got here, to The Islands."

I looked behind as our island sank beneath the waves and our horizon line changed. It looked like Greece. The saturation on all colour notched up a level with the hills interspersed by a little white villa or two with terracotta tiles.

"You do know where we are, don't you?" Ida continued.

"The Islands. The vault of heaven," I whispered, just not ready to face the old man of physics yet, not quite yet. Ida's knee continued to press into mine.

"A pretty good place to look for love I think."

Chapter 27

different paths

Torches illuminate when you are illuminated within; when your path ahead is clear, but when your path is in shadow, you need more illumination to know where to step. Suddenly, the torch is not enough.

I could have asked for floodlights hanging from the cliff. I couldn't see to sink tent pegs in ground they could never part. Rock. The torch was not enough on its own.

I had faced the mountain with trepidation akin to first days at school when I had only thought the trip would endure in the fall of day. Now I was facing a night on the mountain, or more, as the snows continued to fall like I had never seen before, in September, like I had never seen before in any winter month. When would it stop? Blankets of snow were falling. Gone was the realm of the snowflake.

Espen arrived back. He had climbed on ahead when we realised the wind was just too strong across the ridge for us to get back down, or even know which ridge we were on. It wasn't the mountaineering I was used to; mountaineering on clouds where solid ground looks the same as fluid or gaping. Gladness filled me. As long as Espen was back, then we could go on together.

He shook his head and tried to shift more stones onto the sides of the tent to hold it down.

He hadn't found a wider ledge, a ledge as wide as our tent. This was it; this was the spot where we would wait for The Storm to end. The tent wasn't designed for five people. If you positioned five people horizontally across its ground sheet then they fitted like a new pillow in its plastic wrapper; desperate to do what foam does best - expand. And our ledge was not as wide as the ground sheet had potential to be.

I pretended that we were on our way to a party, transporting more bodies than the car had seats for people to be seated in. This way meant there was something at the end of it, that there was a purpose, something to be excited about. Not that I liked parties much. Beer tasted of beer. Cigarettes tasted of cigarettes. My bed was always too far away when I wanted to sleep. But even things you don't like can create excitement as it's all new experience.

Newness to add shine to elements which can grow oxide quickly.

We even had coffee and chocolate in the car, so I was happy. Two of the things I would travel the furthest for. All queues distressed me, made me think time was about to end, that New York would live up to its Hollywood scripts.

But not queues for coffee or chocolate. Those queues I could stand in, idle, not letting the engine rev when it couldn't get you there any quicker if it did.

Why couldn't I approach other aspects of life in the same way? The wait for the job which would fulfil. The wait for the house that could become home. The wait for the person to share home with. My engine was never idle thinking of those things. It was revving away, flexing the clutch but never moving forward.

The last sip of coffee floated the last chunk of chocolate down. My idle engine purred.

We were stuck in a tent with no solid food while rocks and avalanches fell all around and the wind tried to make humans fly from a storm of ferocity the like of which I had never seen. Not in any season. Not in any land. This could now be heralded as The

Storm. Just like some people can be declared The Love and some battles The War.

"What do you really think of Andrea?" asked Espen.

Andrea was asleep, or at least wanted the world to forget about her for some hours, to occupy its time with another.

Sara was hugging oak, the great branches of Nielsen's forearms doing their best to shield what could dent.

Espen believed no one could hear his whisper and therefore I believed that to be certain, for his voice knew its tone more precisely than the violinist in the touring orchestra feels their strings proclaim.

"I feel able to just be me, in all situations. I mean, things aren't perfect; she will tidy what is already sorted and such like. But all have niggles, sent to shave and make us smoother. I could just close my front door now with her inside."

"But?" I responded. There was a weight on his tone now, bringing it down, making it harder to hear.

"Her values aren't always the same as mine; I mean what she believes in when we talk about the big stuff. I need to share everything and for her to feel I am sharing everything."

I sighed. The precursor to my response, the same response I always gave to questions of the big mysteries within.

"You never know quite what is in someone's heart. She might express it in a different way or treat some situations and people differently to you, but you don't know exactly what the foundation is as we all express ourselves a little differently. To build a life together which becomes one of those foundations shouldn't be overlooked. You do less crazy things nowadays and say thank you more than before. I think she is a firm foundation and rock is far better than sand."

I could see Espen thinking about their differences, trying to work out if they mattered enough when he clearly knew that he was happier now than in the days when every moment was a search for a high; through driving fast, climbing high, or pushing to the limit. He had become the person usually giving me advice, telling me to slow down and rest in my pursuit for goals, as he had found greater rest and knew of its properties.

His eyes began to close. Sleep was being summoned from its French Literature class. I had given him hope as I felt that was what he had asked for. Dreams without hope are nightmares. The dress the girl sees in the designer shop and yearns over, yearns over to be pretty for her chap should not be described as *oh I can dream*. Her chap should buy it for her, one day. Then she can dream with that hope inside.

I woke before even the noise could wake me. For a moment it sounded like my father making a trip to the bathroom and never quite finding the light switch. And then I heard it for what it was; a roaring ocean swell, readying to re-carve my beach by morning.

Avalanche.

There wasn't time to even find a zip that had bound heat and now bound our ankles. The tent collapsed. Its protective exoskeleton became spears.

"So I did die in the tent. We all did," I said as the salt spray continued to comb my hair wildly. "And you never rescued us in a helicopter, perhaps you cannot even fly..."

Arlanda couldn't hear. The boat-made wind carried it away. Perhaps it had always been one of his dreams to be a pilot and shattered dreams are never a good thing.

I felt a couple of fingers glance my shoulder. Ida? I would have turned her way, I wanted to turn her way but I let a crack shoot across the glass facade of my dream. The skin had been rough. Age had turned plains into grand valleys. The old man who drove the boat wanted to speak to me. I leant back. He was already bent forward.

"I can see you're one full of doubt. I have seen too many to not know and I was one once. I guess you're sifting through your past. And fragments aren't coming quite together..."

"They will never fit. I don't know what happened to me, I don't know which is the truth..."

"There is only one truth; the rest is lies or make-believe, just stories."

"So, how did I get here? Did I freeze to death in the tent? Did an avalanche sweep me a thousand feet down the mountain? Did my neck break in a helicopter crash? Did I collapse on a mountain ridge?"

"Does it matter how you got here, does it really? Here will be better than anywhere you have been. You have to believe without seeing it first, you are trying to see it first and there is much darkness inside you and so darkness is what you can see."

"Whereas here there is only light?"

"Only light, exactly. And only warmth. No snow and no storms. Now, time to get on your way, we are here. The main island. Time to leave an old man to sleep under his newspaper again."

The boat slid into the beach and broke through the surf. Arlanda and Ida hopped out. Full of energy and lightness as their atoms seemed to be losing weight, becoming helium and soon hydrogen. I was still mostly carbon.

"It all happened," croaked the old man as his grey hair slid from view down into the bottom of the boat where he was now lying. "All your memories happened, but there is only one path you can choose. Everything forks at the end, but only one path..."

I looked back at the others. Ida's hair had more curls and skin more freckles and her hops were more of a dance along the beach. She looked as if she had had ten years of heavy memories taken off.

Arlanda's hair was brown. The brown of a good leather and the little weight around his waist he had been carrying was gone. He was slim. Athletic if not an athlete.

They were becoming younger.

I looked at myself. I could feel the same aches and pains, indeed, my knees ached a little more and there was a heavier feel to the top of my cheeks; where the skin had accumulated like sediment from the flow of rivers.

I was ageing.

Chapter 28

lost

The tea was sweet and cup more a glass without a handle. I could still see some of the leaves which must have given flavour; given what was on the inside to the water.

Why couldn't I just give what was on the inside of me to flavour life? I was acting more like a cola than a tea. Taking from the environment; using eight litres to produce one.

"You suddenly aren't carefree anymore," said Ida, who seemed so content now, sat in the café which was no more than a stone patio and canvas roof spilling onto the beach.

"You are the one who had made me restless back on our first island. I was content doing nothing then..."

"But you shouldn't have been, there is Evelyn to find and also a guy called Nikolai. We have to find him. Doing nothing and being carefree are two completely different things. If you do nothing, you are often trying to bury your worries, whereas carefree should be called worry-free."

"We have to find Nikolai...me? What is wrong with the one we already have?"

"I can see it in your skin...you look like your years and we are getting younger. This is what The Islands are doing to us, but not to you. Some worries somewhere inside, are stopping you being young again. I want to help you."

"I need to help Arlanda find Evelyn and I have to bring with me my friends from the hotel, but then at times it feels like I was never there; that I died in the tent and never lost Espen, instead, lost everyone."

Ida placed her chin in her hands which in turn were propped up on the wooden table, built of driftwood.

"You are helping Arlanda. He isn't here alone. Look at him, he is miles from her and yet he is happy as he has company on his journey as we have travelled together to a café all stop at. He is describing Evelyn to the tea-boy right now. Soon he will be headed her way. You have kept your promise, no doubt. And as for this hotel in the mountains...and your friends...maybe the tea-boy saw them all pass through and you can be carefree again, knowing that you don't have to go back for them..."

"And what if they didn't and they are in danger at the hotel still, or stuck in an avalanche, or injured after a helicopter crash?"

"Then you have me to get to know. One-way ticket Nikolai...one-way. I have left everyone too, or been left behind. I could ponder about what happened to me...did I really walk outside into a storm to clear my steps...or did I fall asleep on the sofa that night...or did I never make it back from the hospital? I can't remember my shift ending, maybe it never did. I choose to be carefree and not worry. I cannot change the past or the future by worrying alone. I don't need to find anyone, but now I have found you to think about, to wonder if you are taller than me and could carry me along the beach sometimes and drive me places if we ever find a car again."

"What did the tea-boy say?" I asked Arlanda. I understood what Ida was trying to say. I wanted to be swept along and maybe just think about her but I couldn't. That was me. That was the way I was made. I had to think about everything, all at once and conclude everything otherwise I wouldn't have a conclusion.

"She drank tea here just like us. The boy knows that as she left a message for me. She is waiting at the foot of the steps to the Great Cathedral on this island. There is a mountain hike between us, that is all. She is waiting for me Nikolai, waiting for me..."

"What with a tall blonde Norwegian called Espen, did you see him? Maybe with three friends?"

The little boy put down his tray and smiled. I could see that he remembered him.

"Yes, he was here, Espen, but not tall, hardly any taller than me and we played for hours on the beach, building a dam before he had to travel on. He was alone and left only a message for Andrea. You aren't Andrea so I can't give you the message."

"So he became young too? Why can't I? And why wasn't he so worried about us not to continue? The others, they are still stuck at the mountain hotel with the soldiers of hell descending the mountain with Andrea captured. I have to go back. I have to go back to get them."

There was a loud crash as the tea-tray clattered on the stone floor, sending remnants of tea over our feet.

"No one goes back...no one. You cannot do this! I have to give a message to Frida, she has to know this."

The boy was now a young man. Worry was ripping through dams built on a beach just for fun. They had been ripped down and the flood waters of worry rushed through him. He was sprinting across the beach back to the blue boat.

Ida's hands slipped over her face. She knew I was heading downstream towards the waterfall and there was nothing much that could stop me.

"You've near as well found her now," I said to Arlanda, relinquishing that responsibility, "She is waiting for you, go to her."

I got up to my feet, trying to make it count more.

"Go, I will go with him," Ida said to Arlanda. He dropped his head and for a moment he was bald again. Ida turned to me.

"Now what, we just swim for it?"

She might have said she would come with me but she was leaving behind the shoes in the sale which she would look so nice in. She was angry that I would just not live for today, believing in the blue sky so blue because that was how it had always been.

Regret is a narrow alleyway. You never know how dark and narrow it is until you look up to see the letterbox of sky-light. It was too long before I looked up. My head had been down and my stride wide as I sprinted down the beach and into the surf. Soon I was waist high and swimming. After ten minutes, I could no longer see the beach when I finally looked up and out of the narrow alley I had been in.

I was in the middle of vast ocean, drifting. I wanted to go back but my arms were tired. They never did that kind of aerobic exercise. Typing on the keyboard required little bicep and tricep training. I wanted to go back but I only drifted away from the beach that was maybe viewable from one wave away, but not mine.

I was cold. As if the fridge door had been left open and was dissipating its heat outside of the room it cooled; my body. A cloud covered the sun. The first cloud I had seen. Within another half hour the sky was grey and it was dusk.

I felt rain followed by the white sprinkles of snow. This was the last thing I saw as I sank under a large wave. I kicked with all my might.

I thought about Ida, about her wonderful smile that lit up my small world, she created a wonderful atmosphere while on the beach and between islands, she had a heart of only goodness and a heart that wanted to serve others, like Arlanda and me. She treated her new friends like closest family and she waited patiently in the beachside café as we hurled logs into the surf. The little children in the café reached out to her with sister-sense arms. I missed her even as I sat on the boat lost in my own memories of entangled events. She was someone who appreciated simple things, the things that did not cost a lot but were full of richness; like our time. She simply made me happy and no one ever had before, not in that way, not in such a short amount of time.

As I sank deeper and kicked less, I realised that the way I felt about Ida was the way The Pilot, Lothen, had described his wife Evelyn when he woke up in the hotel.

That reality, that fork in the road was disappearing into just my imagination in sleep or comatose mode.

It never happened. That description was now my own; the way I felt about Ida or would have come to feel about her if I had just not needed to resolve every equation that the old man of physics set. Some are fine left for the old man of physics to answer.

I tried to breath but I couldn't. My body stopped me swallowing water. I coughed as if the strongest strain of bronchitis had smothered my lungs.

It was night, but I knew it when I felt it. Bed sheets from a hotel, crisp as tissue paper, strong as silk.

I had had my wish. I was back in the mountain hotel; in room seventeen, as if I had never left it.

Chapter 29

yoke

Faith is an egg which you are boiling. On the inside all kinds of things are happening from the heat. The protein strings get so excited that what once flowed as liquid becomes solid and opaque. Faith is the same, as you cannot see what is happening inside the egg to make a judgement on when to take it out of the water. You have to believe in how long the cook book says if you want it dippy for soldiers or hard for good sandwiches. Else you will take it out prematurely, and the buttered soldiers will dip into the clear protein juice which may or may not harbour salmonella.

That was what happened to me. I took the egg out of the pan prematurely, not believing that it needed four and a half minutes at sea level. I had doubted that my friends were safe. I had lost Faith in the master egg chef.

I looked out of the window at the dark expanse of mountain. The mountains shielding the first glimpses of dawn that would have otherwise mellowed the black of centuries. I was back in The Dark Place. But The Storm had passed. The air was no longer full of the hair spray for nature; that binds trees and rock into a firm winter-hold. Indeed, there were specks of water on the window. There had been a mass-extinction. Ice-crystals had been given their chance to flourish and express themselves in symmetrical art but it was all futile; they had now melted and died.

Once the morning came, once daylight revealed the path I had chosen, once I had established whether I was a guest, unwanted or invited; I would be on my way down the valley and the next and could maybe get a run in on the streets of Grünerløkka, Oslo, by evening.

I flicked on the light over the sink in the bathroom and splashed water where I liked it best; where I could not survive without it cleansing my face. Looking up and into the mirror I saw greyness. In my beard. In my hair. Under my eyes. The wood cladding of my house had been re-painted and the colour chosen was grey. I was older now, maybe five years, maybe ten. I wasn't shocked at my appearance. I knew it would come. You cannot stop time. A train without a driver, a feather on the track cannot possibly stop it. But I was shocked at not having a memory of the years that had etched more than any others on my appearance.

I put on a jumper, grey with red diamonds on the front. I wouldn't have chosen it. Now I had. I had gone shopping for a jumper, seen that one on display and decided that it suited me and it became the jumper of the day.

The stairs down to the ground floor felt the same, but creaked more. The timbers more relaxed now after time to settle in. There were lights on downstairs. The kind of lights you put on when you have switched all others off. The front door wasn't barricaded with furniture and the ruffles in the cushions of the cosy corner next to the entrance had been ironed out. All was smooth and tidy. Through the narrow windows either side of the front door I could see a little across the front veranda and steps. There was no snow, not even a sprinkling. It had all melted away, not just the first snowflakes in the front-line against oncoming positive degrees.

I heard a cupboard open or close. The sharp snap of a fastener.

"Nikolai?"

They were standing behind the reception counter, refilling what had been empty, or looting what was worth taking.

"You're up early. Did the sleep help, has your memory of the accident returned?" she continued. Her name badge said *Frida, Reception*. She smiled a perfect smile as she spoke, her tone calming as her large eyelashes created a little breeze between us.

"What accident?" I said as I glanced over at the newspaper on the counter. Tuesday eighth September 2009. Today must have been the nineth. "Seven years," I whispered to myself, "It has been seven years."

"You did warn me that your memory can come and go. You came here to remember what happened to you in the accident, remember? You were the only survivor of the helicopter crash after The Storm seven years ago. You were found by the Norwegian Air Force who were stranded in The Storm. You came back here to try to remember more as it is important that you do, as the only survivor, the only one who endured the crash and the only one who can say what happened."

"What is of great importance that I have to remember?"

"The people who just disappeared. The bodies that were never accounted for. You have to remember what happened to them. A climber called Espen. The pilot of the search and rescue helicopter and his wife, Evelyn..."

"Well, coming back has so far not helped me," I hurriedly replied. I was now an outsider in my own life. What had felt like a prison before had been freedom.

I wished I'd stayed with Ida and found Espen to tell me to rest now. I had woken up in hell with nothing familiar to me. I could still taste the last tea I had drunk. Remnants were flavouring the saliva that rinsed my mouth.

"When is the first bus to Oslo?" I asked.

Frida looked up from typing on the keyboard. Had she just engrained my consciousness thus that she became the flight attendant within my travels to The Islands? Was all that experience just the defragmenting of other memories while my brain switched off and on again? Her appearance matched.

Her voice soothed the same, like lotion that is cold at first.

"Seven O'clock the first bus to Sogndal will pass. There is then a further connection to Oslo..."

"Is there a bus to The Islands?"

"What Islands?" she asked, "Lofoten?"

I wanted her to acknowledge that they existed, even if I could not go there. I wanted to know that such a place did actually exist and Ida would be there still, punching kung fu kicks into the coca-cola surf. Espen - I missed my safety rope and the rope was coiling without me. And I was falling.

My luggage was light. A few jumpers which bridged the gap between young and old; half covered by traditional-dad-jumper pattern. I seemed to have acquired a jumper fondness I never knew was in me as otherwise I only had one shirt and one set of underwear packed.

Maybe I now felt the cold more. Warmth had left my life.

Every minute past seven I felt as if the bus had gone. Even though I had been waiting on the steps since well before seven, staring at the V-shaped spine of mountains, the feeling of having missed the bus remained. The bus came early. I was late. Or, it simply wasn't going to come at all.

There had been no definitive clues in my suitcase to what I would be returning to. No red cross like a photograph of Ida. No paraphernalia from previous travels accumulated in zippy compartments. I didn't even have a bank card with me. Just cash. Around five thousand kroner in notes. Enough for a week or so of life.

The four lights weaved down the mountain. Occasionally they blinked out of view behind one of the false ridges or shone brighter when straight into my eyes.

The bus was finally illuminated with its own shadow behind it and four headlights cloaking it in halogen highlights. All paths led to the hotel steps. The last corner was navigated and the full weight of my bag elongated my arm as it was lifted up from the ground and I took one step forwards. My other arm lifted up. My hand did not wave, just pointed. It was a call to stop as my body entered the internationally accepted position to hail a bus.

Had the mountain bus weaving its way down the pass prompted my vision of the men descending the mountain? It would have been a common sight after dark or before dawn during the shortening September day.

Having paid, I sat down and waited. I had to pay for all transport in this life, everything. The hotel bed. The breakfast I had left before eating. It all cost something. I didn't like that. I wanted to be dozing on a beach with a fountain for my drinks. That was where I had begun to feel young again. I had forgotten about things I had seen as an adult and remembered what I had seen as a child.

Bees for the first time, doing their dancing flight like yo-yos.

Summer where grass had grown taller than my own knees.

And the way cold milk tasted with biscuits when the time had passed the time for sleep. I could remember the taste and see the crumbling of the biscuits on the kitchen table.

All of this I had not just recalled, but relived, as clear as mountain springs. Gone was the silt that slowed my current down and made for stagnancy. As I sat and waited for the journey to pass, I could feel the silt again. Clogging up pure thoughts. Why did the helicopter really crash? Had it been my fault? Did Espen really walk out into the full force of The Storm? Had my comments about Andrea driven him to that? Had something else, or had he really travelled to The Islands; the ninth vault of heaven, where God's light resides.

"Where is God today, on holiday in His villa in Malaga?" I asked myself as anger bubbled away; the first steam reaching the surface.

All steam must be vented. Even volcanoes are not immune.

Someone coughed. There was an old man one row back on the right. As he was behind me I could not see him, but I could hear his strained breathing and he only needed a flaky blue painted boat to complete my memory of him.

"He's not in this place son. Left it long ago. Not been here for years, ever since we discovered how to make bombs and wanted what someone else owned. All cultures think the world will end one day by judgement, fire or famine. All cultures translate their own birth and death to the world they live in. So, we have many beginnings and many ends, but what they don't know is that it has already ended. God left long ago for the soldiers of hell to reoccupy their land. The modern world is the end, nothing you can do 'bout that."

I looked round and the seat reclined, and the old man with clotted wiry grey hair that once maybe cleaned the inside of blackened pans, covered his face with a newspaper.

Anger evolved. Natural selection chose the stronger to prosper. Purpose. A desire for spring to reign and not winter. A desire to grow back stronger what had died.

I had to find a way back to The Islands. To find Ida again would bring joy, if given the chance we could have had beautiful children and chosen pretty names. To find Espen again would bring friendship, if given the chance we could have climbed to the highest heights together.

Anger evolved. My purpose was to find rest. The kind of rest I had as a child after having had cold milk and biscuits and cleaned my teeth in bed from a brown plastic mug stained with toothpaste lava. Oslo would hold my answers. I had not found my memory of events from the helicopter crash on returning to the mountain hotel as that was not where the crash really happened. That was where the debris had been found. But the crash, my crash had begun years before, as I had crossed the rope bridge from being a child to being an adult. And that rope bridge was in Oslo.

Chapter 30

oslo

Day was disappearing like it always did. The betrayal followed by regret the following day. The low light took faces all around and placed a vale over them; lessening the details that make people stand-out as beautiful or not. Everything was smudged charcoal.

Oslo Central Station. Oslo S. 4.54pm on a Wednesday evening late in September. There were briefcases, overcoats, shaded glasses, international newspapers, skis in ski-shaped carrying apparatus, hats of wool and hats of little insulating value, mobile phones with internet access, mobile phones without, an internet café which was empty and one abandoned bag in dark blue, no logos, just a piece of frayed string where once a name and address label might have lived.

This was Oslo S as I walked as quickly as I could under the high ceilings that envelope grand capital stations.

My fingers felt the coins and paper in my pocket. All there, I thought. Perhaps a coin or two could still be on the bus seat, or stuck in the dip between seats where it would remain a long time sheltered in the moist dark. If a seed, the coins would have grown into mighty trees, but money never grows from the unploughed furrow. It remains infertile. The only seed sown is that of pain.

I needed a drink. Something to soften my cracked soil - lips. There had been a vending machine on the way from the bus bay but there had been someone searching for the correct change or any change and I had calculated that it was better to use more time to find somewhere else than just wait in the queue. I couldn't queue. I had been born with that gene missing. Just before the queue I would be relaxed, as calm as when about to sleep to the sound of a river with gentle torrent. Once in the queue, once I had pushed out into the torrent I would remember a place I would have to be, an arrangement that had been arranged now and the queue would abstain from moving quickly to ease my keeping of time. So I had chosen to walk on as that felt like I was achieving something, even though in all likelihood I would use more time searching for something to laminate what had become parched.

It was good to move anyhow after seven hours of cryogenic experimentation. The wonder of what happens to the human body when sat stationery for abnormally long. Things become numb. Other things tingle. Overall you are not sure which bits have any feeling anymore. But it was a small price to pay for the window seat all journey long and the dreams that came from the blurred close-up landscape.

It would take twenty minutes to reach the apartment. No-one would greet me with a glass of something, a warm towel or random object picked up from the dining table. Sometimes a newspaper. Sometimes a photograph. Sometimes something better left on the kitchen table. I had lived alone for long enough to have a cupboard full of cereal boxes. All with remnants of cereal within. All still valued as saviours on the day of no breakfast cereal.

Someone had been coming out as I had come in. So I hadn't needed to enter the code. One, one, two, eight. It had been the code for so long that I had used it as the pin for all cards and even thought it was my birthday at times.

I searched my pockets and everything that had had a pocket sewn into their fabric. There was no key to be found. Had I left it at the mountain hotel? A little sweat made globules as if mercury on my forehead. Glistening silver. I had dismissed the hotel as just the debris of the crash, my crash and not the source, not where the key was to be found, but without a key I could not get in and begin covering in the dry furrow where pain openly looked up at the sun. Oslo had to be the answer to untie the knot. Knots can be tough. Seemingly stronger than metal their resistance hardens with time. I didn't have long. I had to get it untied and let the thread of time weave again.

I forced the door with my shoulder. It caved in showing it was hollow inside and so did the door.

I breathed. For the first time since plunging under the waves when swimming away from The Islands it felt. Oxygen replenished. Vats of carbon dioxide were vented.

On the bookshelf in the lounge there were cards. Joy flowed in dykes within my previously desert fields. Some people had remembered an event. A birthday perhaps. A new job. There would be messages wishing me well and the words would be like medicine.

Next to the cards was a photograph in a frame. My parents. They could have maybe cooked for me the next day. Having someone cook for you is like having a payment into your bank account. It credits your life with so much, so much resource to spend.

The white desert of Egypt burst forth in my heart. It had once been a mighty mountain range this desert but harsh winds had eroded the soft rock into mere nodules drowning in newly made sand. My rock was now sand.

In the photograph of my parents, one hanging onto blonde, one nearing the time that noses and earlobes hit their growth spurt, there was their son. Held like only a son is held.

It wasn't me.

It was someone else.

Not as handsome. Perhaps unable to draw tiny people on tiny paintings.

I heard someone arrive home and stop at a door which should have been closed.

Chapter 31

one way

"Even cats that go missing get a poster," I thought.

The chair squeaked as the police officer shifted from side to side.

There were four of them in the room. It was a quiet night or my siren blazed louder than they had heard for a while. Their faces were all stern, looks that had a precise purpose with no room for jollity.

"So let's go through this again, which one are you?"

"Nikolai," I answered the officer in the chair, for a moment I was sure he looked identical to the maths teacher who had subtracted much from my learning and added nothing. For a moment he was a demon from my early years, someone who had made me feel I was not up to the grade and once I had felt that, I had lost my footing on the giant conveyor belt of passage to getting a delivery stamp and progressing to my final destination. The moment passed. I looked closer and he actually had a thick beard and was far too tall, even when sat. Even when sat I felt I was not as tall if I stood.

"We have looked up this accident you speak about. And it happened the night of a great storm in the region. Five people died, Espen, Lothen, Sara, Nielsen and Andrea. The people you tell of. The fire must have been so severe from the crash as they only ever found the remains of three. Espen and Lothen's bodies were never recovered, although some personal artefacts were. What we want to know is why you think you were there. We have no record of that. There were no survivors."

He glanced down at the piece of paper in his hands with pencil scribbles on, folded many times and not in a planned way like origami.

"You're not on the list," he continued. "And then there is the case of this evening. The case of breaking into Nikolai and Natalie's apartment..."

He had been a wimp. If it had been me I would have at least boiled a little on the inside and spat out a few ridiculous punches. But he had just dropped his shopping and his girlfriend's hand. He had introduced himself as Nikolai and she had phoned the police. I hadn't tried to make excuses like making a routine radon gas level reading. One of the cards had been handmade. A series of phrases written in delicate handwriting that looped in arcs, following unseen contours that had maybe been sketched in pencil beforehand. The result was a picture made up of words. A crowd of people facing one man who had been masked out so they were made up out of only the paper beneath which appeared as light.

In 1988 I had seen a little girl sketch something similar, but the gaps between words and sentences hadn't been so BMW. The precision just hadn't been there. But I recognised the drawing all the same. She had drawn it just before we opened the rabbit hutch and put the rabbit in the transport cage for the Easter holidays.

I had felt like I had deserted my friends; that by travelling to The Islands alone I had betrayed them, but now I could help them even less. Our threads had unravelled and the ladies knitting the Norwegian woollen socks of winter legend had stopped knitting. I could remember meeting Andrea for the first time at Bocata and her comments about my T-Shirt. Nudie. Grey but an interesting grey. A little mottled from the ravages of the war with the washing machine. A little nick from the hamster that lived in the closet. A good T-shirt never dies. I remembered the various hats that had become Espen's hat of the day. Knitted. Pink. With flowers. Ear flaps. At home in a silent movie. Given the fright of their lives, these hats had never seen such a thing as they were taken up extremities when they had been designed for Oxford boating trips.

I smiled. They were still my friends inside me. Our stages of overlap could never be tugged apart. Therefore I had never deserted them as I had carried them with me; the bits that had been shared.

I should have carried on. Over the mountain. And to the valley that flows from the top of every mountain.

I should have let the wave of Ida flow over me and not let my past disappointments, near-misses and vast wipe-outs be projected onto her. I'd had the chance of wiping chalk off the blackboard and I now rued not taking it for at the other end of a pole is its opposite. North opposing south.

A place where no one loved me. A place where I was not Nikolai anymore.

The chair squeaked as the police officer shifted from side to side.

He had turned his piece of paper over to reveal a new list. His beard gaped wide as a jungle opening to the bat cave.

"There is a new list you are on..."

A lady came into the room and placed a folded item of clothing on the table. It was orange. The orange of a good Clementine where the skin is still tort to the segments.

The jumpsuit which had been in so many of my visions.

A cardboard box was placed next to it.

"Please put your clothes in there. We will have to burn them of course," another officer said, in a voice not as deep but still within the realms of bass that carries into neighbour bedrooms.

"What list am I on?"

"They have no name. They just appear in society without any record of them anywhere. We see them on the news. They are the ones who blow up buildings and bury seventeen people in their back gardens. If anything, they can only be described as the soldiers of hell. Luckily we have caught you early...before..."

The face remained stern. There wasn't even the slightest secretion on his skin to reflect a little light my way.

So, I turned to the woman who had come in carrying my new clothing, complete with a detainee number on the sleeve. Her hair was black and tied tightly back. Her large eyelashes coiled as if spring loaded. I had seen her teeth when she had breathed consciously. Perfectly aligned teeth had flowed into river bank gums.

Frida, Officer 4995

"I want to go back to The Islands...can you do that? I'm ready now; I'm ready to stay there. You said it was a one-way trip...can you make an exception, this time? I'm not a soldier of hell. I was a good boy who made presents from things he found in the garden..."

Frida looked back blankly but the light caught her skin. Perhaps it was oilier, but light was reflected back at me.

"What Islands?" she said, "Ibiza? Many book one-way tickets. Often cheaper I guess. One-way. One way. Of course...there is another kind of *one way*. If we think about choices and not journeys. Journeys are linear but choices can bring you full circle. One way. One true way."

9 gifts

The Dark Paper Machine

By James Ecendance

(Published by Idearich: ISBN 978-0-9559387-0-2)

James Ecendance's The Dark Paper Machine is first and foremost a thriller which takes the reader, through the eyes of Finn, on a journey to defeat a system of control which threatens the life of his wife and child. This is Ecendance's first published novel and is a culmination of seven year's work. As a thriller the pace is fast and the plot is racy, however Ecendance intertwines a love story. He scatters vivid romantic imagery throughout, which contrasts with the dark undertones of the main storyline, giving the novel captivating depth. He engages the reader's emotions whilst simultaneously holding their interest with the exciting pace of the main plot.

The first chapter opens with Finn's wistful observation that 'the sun was low in the sky but it never rose that high at this time of year'. This is typical of Ecendance's descriptive power which creates a pensive atmosphere throughout the novel. The reason for this mood unfolds quickly as we are taken back three years when Finn awakens on a train in Oslo with the dawning realisation that he has amnesia. Finn's dependency on the Dark Paper Machine is realised as Ecendance writes that 'Every memory requires an anchor. A place that ties memories together. A home, a wood where you played as a child, something of three dimensions that your scenes play within. I had no anchor... The Dark Paper Machine had become my substitute'; the scene is set.

Tension builds as Ecendance introduces members of the machine. The first character we meet is Deluth. She is presented in the first instance as a cold unfeeling character, heavily embedded within the machine; the reader is aloof and unattached to Deluth. She is seen as frightening but flat and cold. Primarily Deluth is presented as 'having a confident poise in her shoulders', with 'her lips rigid and stern' an emotionless character much like other members of control who have 'shaven heads' and whose 'eyes are back and piercing'. As the story unfolds however, Ecendance further develops her character by revealing to the reader her feelings for Finn in an emotionally charged and touching scene. The reader is asked to re-evaluate Deluth and although she is still not a likeable character, pity is evoked. We see the humanity present within the structure of the machine which adds soul to the image of the Dark

Paper Machine. The reader is drawn to the truly terrible and destructive nature of this system which seeks to prevent all human emotion, weakness and fragility. The effect is chilling.

Ecendance weaves contrast throughout the novel. He plays with ideas of time and distance through Finn's flashbacks of his old life with Nina, making for a tense and fast paced read. Nina has no physical presence within the novel; she is played out in her entirety through Finn's memory and imagination. She exists within Finn. Nina also serves to give the reader insight into Finn's character. We learn through Nina of Finn's ability to lose himself in dreams and memories, his admiration of the little things in life and the simplicity of his hopes and desires. Simultaneously showing us his greatest fear; losing her 'it didn't feel like she was touching me, comforting me, telling me that everything would be alright. I slid down the wall where I had been standing and crouched.' Whilst Finn serves as a mirror into Nina's character, Finn is mirrored within her, again strengthening and communicating the idea that love will be the downfall of the Dark Paper Machine.

The fluidity of Ecendance's ideology is apparent throughout. The idea of Nina and Finn existing within one another is echoed in his descriptive prose; 'The opera house glittered white in the harbour, the marble reflecting the shimmering waters and the waters reflecting the angular mountain', This interweaving and repetition of similar ideas occurs continuously throughout the novel. Numerous parallels can be drawn within the narrative that are free flowing, lucid and graceful.

As Finn is overwhelmed by flashbacks, his love for Nina is used as the driving force in challenging The Dark Paper Machine. Nina is described vividly and emotively;

'her eyes were the colour of a great autumn, where the leaves turn the richest brown you never thought existed. She did not walk or run but floated like the weightless leaves themselves... '

These descriptions are at the heart of the novel and Ecendance creates a bitter sweet tone by combining Finn's aching and intense yearning to be reunited with Nina to the light romantic depictions of the life they used to share. By entangling Nina and Finn's identity, a defence against The Dark Paper Machine is introduced. The reader is swept into the drama of

Finn's mission to 'find a 3D fragment from my flash-backs, then perhaps my need for them, to be sheltered by them, the machine, would break'.

Available at **www.idearich.com**

Author's Note:

Thank you for buying my second novel. Thank you to the people who believe in me and a big thank you to Suzy.